CHARMING A FAIRYTALE COWBOY

Copyright © August 2022 by Katie Lane

All rights reserved. Except for use in any review, the reproduction or utilization of this work in whole or in part in any form by any electronic, mechanical or other means, now known or hereinafter invented, including xerography, photocopying and recording, or in any information storage or retrieval system, is forbidden without the written permission of the publisher.

This book is a work of fiction. Names, characters, places, and incidents are a product of the writer's imagination. All rights reserved. Scanning, uploading, and electronic sharing of this book without the permission of the author is unlawful piracy and theft. To obtain permission to excerpt portions of the text, please contact the author at katie@katielanebooks.com Thank you for respecting this author's hard work and livelihood.

Printed in the USA.

Cover Design and Interior Format

Charming a FAIRYTALE COWBOY

Kingman Ranch
·4·

KATIE LANE

*To my feisty little Austin Girl,
Sienna Grace*

Chapter One

THERE WAS RICH.

And then there was filthy rich.

As Shane Ransom stepped out of his beat-up Dodge pickup, he couldn't help staring in open-mouthed awe at the huge stone castle with its turrets that stretched up into the dark Texas night sky.

So this was Buckinghorse Palace. When his brother had first mentioned the name the townsfolk had given the Kingmans' house, Shane had laughed his ass off. But he wasn't laughing now. This *was* a palace fit for a king. After growing up in a rusty trailer with one bathroom, Shane couldn't help feeling envious. But one day, he'd have his own castle on a hill. Come hell or high water.

"Hey, Reverend Ransom!"

Shane turned to find a chubby teenager standing there grinning from ear to ear, the moonlight glinting off his braces. The greeting didn't surprise Shane. Folks confused him for his twin brother, Chance, all the time. But he *was* surprised by the kid's ten-gallon hat and gun and holster.

Noting his confusion, the kid whipped out the plastic gun and fired a few caps into the air. "It's all part of my costume. I'm Hoss from the old TV show *Bonanza*. My grandma loves Hoss."

Shane liked the kid on the spot. Not only because he was a *Bonanza* fan, but also because he had wanted to make his grandma happy.

"Grandmas should be catered to for the short time they are on this earth," he said. Something Shane wished he'd learned sooner.

The kid slipped the toy gun back in his holster. "If you give me your keys, I'll park your truck. The Kingmans don't want people parking in front." Shane tossed him his keys and the kid gave him a valet stub. As he hopped behind the wheel, the teenager shook his head. "I thought a preacher would drive something fancier."

Shane quoted a Bible scripture his grandma had always quoted whenever he asked for something they couldn't afford. "'For we brought nothing into this world, and it is certain we can carry nothing out.'" When the kid looked even more confused, Shane laughed. "You're right. It's a piece of shit truck."

The kid's mouth dropped open in shock and Shane should've told him he wasn't a preacher. But while Chance was a saint, Shane had always been a little bit of a devil. Pretending to be his brother was one of his favorite things to do. So he only winked before he headed toward the castle.

At the huge oak front doors with their intricately engraved *K*'s, Shane rang the doorbell, then stood back to wait. When several minutes passed, he figured the doorbell couldn't be heard over the loud country music and laughter coming from the house, so he opened the door and stepped inside.

The inside was as impressive as the outside. The foyer had polished marble floors and a high ceiling with a domed skylight. From the skylight hung a glistening chandelier with gold prancing horses intermingled with the dangling crystals. The foyer was filled with people all dressed in western costumes.

There was no way Shane was going to find his brother in this crowd.

He pulled out his cellphone and texted Chance. I'm here. Where are you?

A second later, his phone pinged with a reply.

Forgot to set the church alarm. Had to run back to town. Do NOT go inside until I get back. Dots appeared on the screen before another text came in. I mean it, Shane. I don't want you causing any more confusion than you already have.

Shane smiled as he texted back.

You know I live to confuse people. He could almost see his brother gritting his teeth. Shane figured he'd screwed with Chance enough and quickly texted again. I'll wait for you out front.

He pocketed his phone and went to leave when a woman's voice stopped him.

"Reverend Ransom!"

He glanced over his shoulder to see a short, stocky woman in an old-fashioned women's riding costume hurrying toward him. In the brown wig, it took him a moment to recognize Kitty

Carson. When he did, he mentally groaned. Chance had wanted him to stay under the town's radar until he could officially introduce him. Unfortunately, Kitty *was* the town's radar. She not only delivered mail to the town of Cursed, Texas, she also delivered all its gossip.

He pinned on a smile. "Well, hey, Ms. Carson. How are you?"

She put a hand on her hip and flashed a bucktoothed grin. "I'm Annie Oakley tonight. I wanted to be Miss Kitty from *Gunsmoke*, but the bridal attendants are all wearing saloon girl costumes." While he tried to figure out how a wedding fit into a charity ball, she gave him the once-over. "Kayce from *Yellowstone*? Although that's not an old western. And isn't his character a little violent for a preacher?"

It looked like he was going to have to come clean. "I'm not really a preacher. I'm Chance's—"

Before he could say *brother*, her eyes narrowed on something over his shoulder. "The gall of that woman! I'm glad you're taking over for Reverend Floyd. The man refused to do anything about Hester Malone. But I know you're not the type of man who will let a witch continue to practice her witchcraft in our godly town."

Shane turned to see a tall, gray-haired woman in a flowing black dress talking with a man dressed like John Wayne. Hester Malone was the town fortune-teller and palm reader. While Shane didn't believe in that kind of hocus-pocus, he had to admit the woman was intuitive. She was the only one who had seen through the twin switch Shane had pulled. Even now, when she glanced over, her eyes narrowed. Of course, that could have to do with Kitty. The two women did not get along.

"See what I mean?" Kitty said. "She's trying to curse me with her evil eye right now. If that isn't the sign of a witch, I don't know what is." Before he could figure out how to reply to such craziness, Kitty ducked into the large room off the foyer.

Shane glanced back at Hester. The woman *did* have a penetrating stare. When she started toward him, he figured now was a good time to duck out like Kitty.

Once outside, he glanced around. To the right of the castle was an elaborate garden with all kinds of trees, plants, and flowers, and a quaint cottage that looked like it came right out of a storybook. Granny Ran would've loved it. She might have lived in a rusted old trailer, but she had grown the most beautiful flowers and biggest vegetables at the trailer park.

With some time to kill before Chance got there, he decided to take a stroll in the garden. The path was lined with bronze statues of the championship horses raised on the ranch. There were quite a few. Shane stopped to read the names of each horse before he came to the stone steps at the end of the path. He followed them down to a hedge maze. As a kid, he hadn't been able to afford expensive video games, but his grandmother had gotten him and Chance a *Pac-Man* game at a thrift store. Chance hadn't cared for it, but Shane had loved getting that munching dot through the maze. So he didn't hesitate to enter the labyrinth. He was somewhere in the middle when he noticed the sound of trickling water. He followed it to a break in the hedge. When he stepped through, the sight that greeted him took him by surprised.

It was a secret garden complete with a lush lawn, vibrant spring flowers, a beautiful tile fountain with cascading water . . . and a garden fairy.

Although the woman who sat on the edge of the fountain with her feet dangling in the moonlit pool of water didn't look like a fairy as much as a siren. Her red saloon girl dress was hiked up to her knees, showing off shapely legs. Her dark curls fell around her shoulders, playing peekaboo with the soft swells of her breasts above the low-cut neckline.

As he watched from the shadow of the hedge, she tossed something into the fountain and paused for a moment. Then she reached for the bottle of champagne sitting on the ledge next to her and took a deep swig. She set the bottle down and released a long sigh.

"Some ball, Karl. I didn't even get asked to dance once."

Shane glanced around for a man, but all he saw was a mean-looking goat munching on some red roses.

The woman splashed her feet in the fountain. "I mean is it too much to ask for a man who has enough guts to ask me to dance?"

Shane moved out of the shadow of the hedge

and took off his cowboy hat. "Beautiful women are intimidating."

The woman startled and placed a hand on her chest. "Jesus!" He was about to apologize for scaring her when her eyes widened. "You." He thought she had mistaken him for his brother . . . until she continued. "You're the cowboy I kissed at Nasty Jack's bar."

Now he was the one surprised. He stepped closer and studied her features in the moonlight. "You're the pool-playing cowgirl? The one who took all my money?"

She pulled her feet out of the fountain and stood. "I didn't take it. You bet it."

"After you conned me into it."

She sent him the sassy smile that had haunted his dreams for the last few months. "All's unfair in love and pool."

Shane laughed. Suddenly, coming to the Kingman Ranch so his brother could introduce him to the townsfolk of Cursed wasn't such a waste of time. He remembered the night at the only bar in town. He remembered it well. It wasn't because a girl had bested him at pool. It was because after besting him, she had followed him outside and kissed him like no woman had ever kissed him before. He'd wanted more, but the old guy who ran the bar had chased him off with a gun. Still, Shane had thought about that night often and wondered what would've happened if the old man hadn't shown up.

Now he had a chance to find out. If her smile was any indication, she was as happy to see him as he was to see her.

"So what are you doing here?" she asked.

"I was supposed to meet my brother at the Cowboy Ball, but he's running late. So I thought I'd take a look around the infamous Kingman Ranch."

"And what do you think?"

"It's more over the top than I thought it would be. I mean who builds a castle on a Texas ranch?"

Her eyes narrowed. "Maybe a man who can afford to."

So she was just like the rest of the town. The townsfolk of Cursed thought the Kingmans could do no wrong. He understood. From what his brother had told him, the Kingman Ranch employed half the town and helped support the other half.

He held up his hand. "I didn't mean any offense. A castle just seems a little odd for a ranch."

She relaxed and reached out to pet the goat that now didn't look mean as much as lovestruck. It looked up at the woman with big, adoring eyes as she spoke. "I guess it is pretty odd. And wasteful. The money could've been spent on better things."

"Like goats?"

She laughed. "Yes."

"So what are you doing out here when there's a ball going on in a castle?" He hesitated. "I don't believe for a second that no one asked you to dance."

She turned the goat toward the break in the hedge and patted its butt. "Go on now, Karl. You shouldn't be in here eating the roses." When the goat was gone, she looked back at Shane. "It's true. The only ones who asked me to dance were my brothers."

He studied her features in the moonlight. Her hair was as black as a moonless night. Her nose had a cute little tilt on the end. She had the kind of mouth that easily smiled. And expressive eyes that couldn't lie. Right now, they held a sadness that touched his heart.

"Then you have a town of dumbasses." He set his cowboy hat on the fountain ledge and held out his hand. "May I have this dance, miss?"

She lifted her eyebrows. "With no music?"

He cocked his head. "There's music. Don't you hear it? The crickets sound a little off key, but the trickling water is as pitch perfect as any country ballad."

There was a moment when he thought she'd decline. Then she took his hand. She wasn't a small woman. Even shoeless, she was only half a head shorter than he was in his boots. But she seemed to fit perfectly in his arms.

She smelled good. Not like perfume or lotions and hair products. Her scent was simple. Clean soap and something earthy. If the tan on her arms was any indication, she spent a lot of time outdoors—at something that took physical strength. Her arms had definition. He started to ask her what she did for a living, but then stopped himself. The thought of keeping his mystery girl a mystery was titillating.

He waltzed her around the fountain. The fifth

time around, he spun her under his arm before lowering her into a dip. When he set her back on her feet, she swayed and he placed a hand on her waist to steady her.

"You okay?"

She nodded. "The spinning just made me a little dizzy."

"Are you sure it's not the champagne?"

"I didn't drink that much. It was almost empty by the time I got here."

He grinned. "So you're only slightly drunk."

"More like slightly buzzed. But not enough that I couldn't lay you out if you tried something I didn't like."

His gaze locked with hers. At the bar, her cowboy hat had shadowed her eyes so he hadn't been able to tell their color. Now he knew they were a startling blue that reflected the moonlight like twin mountain lakes. In them, he saw the exact need that ate at him.

A need for something more.

Shane lowered his head. "In that case, I'll only do things you like."

Chapter Two

Delaney Kingman's wish had come true.

Not the wish she'd made when she tossed the penny into the fountain—she would never waste a fountain wish on a man—but the wish she'd made every day after being kissed at her uncle's bar.

Hester Malone had been right. Delaney's mystery cowboy had returned.

And his kisses were twice as good as she remembered.

He didn't kiss her with little pecks like John Mumford in third grade. Or awkward mouth-bumps like Anthony Baca's behind the high school bleachers. Or sloppy devouring like Eddie Jones at the Fourth of July hoedown—although Eddie had been drunk as a skunk. This man took his time, with skilled, gentle pulls of his lips and soft sweeps of his tongue. His hands rested at her corseted waist, his thumbs strumming back and forth over the satin of her dress like the hands of a clock ticking off the time until they would move. Finally, they did move. One hand slid around to cradle her butt cheek and one slid up to cradle her breast.

No man had ever touched her like this, and her breath hung suspended in her chest as he reshaped her with his hot palms and agile fingers. It was hard to describe the feelings that rocked her. She felt tingly and energized. And, at the same time, weak kneed and limp. She had never been a weak-kneed kind of woman and the strange languid feeling scared her. What if she had bitten off more than she could chew? What if she wasn't ready for this kind of intense passion?

She drew back from the kiss and rested her forehead on his chin, trying to stabilize her off-balance emotions. He released her breast and bottom and lifted her chin until her gaze met his.

He had pretty eyes. They were the deep brown of a sorrel mare and held a gentleness that was more animal than human. "Are you sure you're okay?" he asked. "Maybe I should drive you home."

The night of their first kiss, he hadn't known she was a Kingman . . . and it looked like he still didn't. But if he had been invited to the Cowboy Ball by his brother, his brother must know her family. And all it would take was the right question to figure out her identity.

Which meant she would never get this opportunity again. Once he learned she was the overprotected sister of the Kingman brothers, he would run for the hills. No man wanted to go up against her three brothers or the Kingman power and wealth. She couldn't see this man being any different. If she wanted more of his knee-weakening kisses, she only had this one chance. Was she going to let a little fear keep her from finally seeing what sex was all about?

She shook her head. "I don't want to go home."

She burrowed her fingers through his thick, wavy hair and drew his mouth back to hers. This time, she took charge of the kiss, molding her lips to his and delving her tongue into the warm recesses of his mouth.

He tasted rich and decadent . . . like dark chocolate. She loved dark chocolate. Almost as much as she loved the way he gave her free rein to kiss him like she wanted to. He didn't try to duel with her tongue or fight for dominance with his lips. He just followed her lead as his hand stroked her back in a soothing up and down caress.

Their kisses grew deeper and more intense. As did the need building inside her. Soon kissing wasn't enough. She wanted more. Much more. She reached for the open neck of his western shirt and tugged open the snaps. She must have tugged a little too hard because a ripping sound rent the air.

She drew back and looked down at his torn shirt. She would have apologized if she hadn't been so distracted by the body beneath the tattered edges of cotton. His shirt wasn't the only thing ripped. His body was too.

Unable to stop herself, Delaney slipped her hand beneath the opening. His stomach muscles jumped as her fingers grazed them. Probably because her hand was cold compared to the heat of his body. She held them against his warm skin until they heated before trailing her fingertips up the center indentation between his abs. When she reached the hollow of his throat, she slid her hands across his collarbone and pushed the shirt off his shoulders.

Her breath escaped her lungs in a huff of surprise and appreciation. She had seen half-naked men before. The ranch hands were always running around without their shirts on. And a time or two, she'd caught them running around with much less. She had looked. Who wouldn't? Some of those cowboys had been pretty hot. But not one of them had made her feel the way she felt now. Breathless. Awed. And a wee bit intimidated.

It wasn't just the multitude of tanned muscles—although those were nice. It was the mixture of his muscles and the sprinkling of chest hair and the white scar that ran along the joint of his shoulder and the tattoo of a royal flush poker hand on his right bicep. His body told a story and Delaney couldn't help wanting to read it with her fingertips.

She traced the puckered scar on his shoulder. "What's this?"

"I tore my rotator cuff playing high school basketball and had to have surgery."

"And this?" She outlined the *A* of the Ace of Diamonds on the round curve of his bicep.

"A college friend talked me into it after too much tequila."

"And you regret it?"

His voice was like rough velvet when he spoke.

"I usually don't regret much."

She lifted her gaze from his tattoo to find him watching her with an intensity that was almost like a physical touch. Then he did touch her. His finger moved slowly and feathery-soft along the elastic neckline of her saloon girl dress. It dipped into her cleavage for a breathless moment before sliding back out and coming to a stop on the swell of her right breast.

She read the question in his deep brown eyes.

Do you want to keep going?

It was a good question. Part of her was scared. But the other part was tired of being the Kingman princess who had been put on a pedestal no man could reach. To this man, she was just a woman. A woman he desired. Even if it was just for one night, Delaney intended to release all the baggage that came with being a Kingman and enjoy the passion of this man.

"Don't stop," she whispered as she pulled his lips to hers.

Their kisses grew hotter and more intense. As he manipulated her desire with his tongue and mouth, his hand pushed down the neckline of her dress and caressed the swells of her breasts above her strapless bra. While she was focused on that magical touch, his other hand unclasped her bra. Once it was gone, he encased her in his large, warm hand and everything inside her melted like a wax candle held to a torch. A second later that melted wax was set aflame when he brushed his thumb over her nipple.

And he wasn't finished.

After he had her nipple tight and achy, he drew back from their kiss and dipped his head to her breast. The feel of him sucking her into his hot, wet mouth had sparks exploding through her body into a cascade of lust and need.

"Oh!" she breathed as she furrowed her fingers through his hair to hold him exactly where he was. He continued to suckle and lick until she trembled with the force of the sensations skittering through her. She wanted more than just his mouth on her breast. She needed more. She tugged his head up and kissed him, hiking her leg around his lean hips and drawing him to the part of her that throbbed for release.

He drew back from the kiss and spoke against her lips. "Easy, sweetheart."

"I don't want easy." She nipped at his bottom lip. "I want you. And I want you now."

His eyes flickered with surprise before they turned to liquid heat. "Where do you want me?" He bunched up the full skirt of her dress and pressed his fingers against her wet panties, causing her breath to suck in. "Here? Do you want me here?"

Her reply came out choked and strangled. "P-P-Please."

He quickly slipped her panties off her hips, then his fingers returned to tease and explore until she moaned deep in her throat and swayed on her feet. Just when she thought she would drop to the ground in a whimpering puddle, he scooped her into his arms and carried her to the fountain. He sat down and arranged her on his lap facing away from him with her dress hiked up and her legs hooked on either side of his muscled thighs. She was totally exposed to the cool night air, but she didn't care when he touched her with his skilled fingers, exploring and delving before he settled into a rhythm that made her lean her head back on his shoulder and moan with pleasure.

With each stroke of his fingers, she became more and more mindless. The orgasm that broke over her in waves was so intense she thought she might black out. Once it was over, he guided her back to reality with gentle strokes and encouraging words.

"I got you, sweetheart. I got you." When she sagged against him, he adjusted her legs, lowered her dress, and tucked her against his warm chest. "You good?"

"Mmm-hmm." She burrowed closer. If she could have climbed into his skin, she would have. She rested there, enjoying the feeling of being in his arms, until two things came to her attention: a pinging noise and the throbbing hardness beneath her bottom.

She lifted her head. "But you're not good."

He grinned. "I think if we want to go further we're going to need a bed. This stone ledge isn't exactly comfortable."

She blinked. "So we're not having sex?"

"Oh, we're having sex. Just not tonight." He gave her a quick kiss before he lifted her to her feet and stood. "I have to meet my brother." He flashed her a smile. "But if you want to wait for me, we could go back to your place later."

She shook her head. "That won't work. Now. We need to have sex now. Otherwise, I might not get another chance." She reached for the button of his jeans and tugged it open. But before she could pull down his zipper, he stopped her.

"Hey, now. We'll get another chance to be together." He took her chin in his hand and lifted her gaze to his. "I promise you."

"No, we won't. Take my word for it. It's now or never."

"Never say never." He kissed her deeply, cradling her breast in his hand and cupping her bare bottom under the skirt of her dress. Just as she was starting to think that maybe they were going to have sex after all, Kitty Carson's voice caused her to freeze.

"You stop chasing me, you beast!"

Delaney drew back from the kiss just as Kitty came running through the break in the hedge with Karl the Goat chasing after her. Both the woman and the goat stopped short when they saw Delaney in the arms of her mystery cowboy.

But it turned out the cowboy wasn't a mystery after all.

At least not to Kitty Carson.

"Reverend Ransom?"

Delaney slowly turned to the man who still held her breast and butt. "You're a preacher?"

He quickly released her and pulled the neckline of her dress over her breasts before he answered. "No. I'm not a preacher."

Kitty gasped. "You're a liar. I just spoke to you. You're just trying to confuse me because you don't want me sounding the alarm that the new preacher of our church is out here in the garden seducing our sweet little Delaney Kingman."

The man turned to Delaney with stunned eyes. "You're a Kingman?"

She felt a twinge of guilt for not telling him sooner. But he hadn't told her who he was either. "You're the new pastor of Holy Gospel?"

"He sure is," Kitty said. "But he won't be for long. Not if I have anything to say about it." She turned and hurried out the break in the hedge.

"Shit," Reverend Ransom cussed. What kind of a preacher cussed? Of course, nothing about the man was preacher like. Not his beer drinking or his pool playing or royal flush tattoo. And especially not his wicked kisses and caresses.

"You're a preacher?" she said again.

"I'm not a preacher." He scooped up his shirt and pulled it on, then cringed when he saw the rip that would make snapping it impossible.

"Then why does Kitty Carson think you are? Did you or did you not talk to her tonight?"

He sighed. "I did, but she mistook me for—"

"Del!"

Delaney froze at the sound of her brother Buck's voice. Then she went into panic mode. "You have to get out of here, and you have to get out of here now." She grabbed his arm and tried to tug him to the opening, but he pulled back.

"I can't leave until I set things straight."

She shook her head. "You don't understand. There's no setting things straight with my brothers. They'll punch first and ask questions later."

"I'm sure they aren't that primitive."

"They're that primitive!" She tugged on his arm. "Now get out of here before—"

Buck came charging through the opening in the hedge. All of her brothers had dressed like cowboy movie stars. Wolfe and Stetson had both chosen John Wayne. Her brother-in-law Gage had chosen Robert Redford as Butch Cassidy. And Buck had dressed like Clint Eastwood in *For a Few Dollars More*. Delaney had to admit he looked pretty badass with his flat-brimmed hat, thick scruff, and Mexican poncho. The fact that his eyes narrowed in anger when he came to a dead halt only added to the Eastwood look.

"Don't you dare come charging in here thinking to play big bad brother, Buck Kingman," she said. "This is none of your business."

"It sure as hell is my business when my sister is carrying on with a perverted pastor." Buck turned his attention to Reverend Ransom. "If you think your profession is going to save you, preacher, you got another think coming." He stripped off his poncho, then started unbuckling his gun holster.

Reverend Ransom held up his hands. "Look, I don't want to fight anyone. This has all been a big misunderstand—"

The rest of Delaney's family arrived. Her oldest brother, Stetson, and his wife, Lily. Her sister, Adeline, and her husband, Gage. Her older brother, Wolfe, and his new wife, Gretchen. Even her great-uncle Jack, who was over eighty, came shuffling in with Kitty Carson. No one looked happy. Probably because Kitty had done what she did best—made everything out to be worse than it was.

Although it *was* pretty bad. Talk about horrible luck. Instead of fooling around with some mystery man who no one knew, she'd fooled around with the new pastor of the only church in town. But since she was never one to confess her crimes, she tried to bluff her way through.

"Hey, y'all. How's the ball going? I was just getting ready to head back to see if you needed any help with the cleanup. But please don't put me on dishwashing duty. You know how I hate to wash—"

"You're right," Stetson cut her off. "You go on back to the house, Del. In fact, all the ladies should go back to the house."

Lily rested her hand on Stetson's arm. She was a little bit of a thing, but she held all the power in their marriage. "Nice try, Stetson, but I'm not leaving you to do something you're going to regret."

Stetson's gaze remained on the pastor. "Believe me, I won't regret it."

"Neither will I," Wolfe growled.

"I'll take the leftovers," Gage said.

"Wait a second," Buck jumped in. "I was here first. If anyone gets to beat the crap out of the preacher, I do."

"No one is going to beat up anyone," Adeline said. "I'm sure there's a good explanation for what Pastor Chance and Delaney were doing here in the maze."

Buck turned to Adeline. "Really, Addie? The guy's shirt is ripped and Delaney's bra is dangling off the fountain. I don't think they were playing lawn croquet."

"They most certainly were not," Kitty piped up. "I saw the preacher mauling sweet little Delaney with my own two eyes. As far as I'm concerned the man should be run out of town on a rail."

Kitty's words made Delaney realize the severity of the situation. This wasn't just about her brothers roughing up the pastor. This was about the entire town turning against him. No one messed with a Kingman and got away with it. And it was her fault. She was the one who'd followed him out into the bar parking lot. The one who'd tempted him with a little sexual fun. The one who'd refused to tell him her name. And now he could lose his job. Not just a job, but also his calling. All because she'd played Eve in the Garden of Kingman. She couldn't let the pastor pay for her sin.

There was only one way she could think of to save him.

She reached out and took his hand, linking their fingers. "I don't know what all the fuss is about. Can't an engaged couple have a little fun?"

Chapter Three

UP UNTIL THIS point, Shane had kept his mouth shut for one reason and one reason only. He was pissed. Not just at Delaney Kingman for not telling him who she was, but also at himself for letting his libido rule his logical brain. He had no business fooling around with a woman whose name he didn't even know. Now he was paying the price.

Engaged? Had she just said they were engaged?

He stared at her and was about to deny her claim when she rambled on.

"Now don't look so surprised, honey buns. I know you wanted us to wait to tell everyone, but I think letting the cat out of the bag is better than getting punched out by my brothers. Wouldn't you agree?" She looked back at her family, who seemed as stunned as Shane was. "So y'all have nothing to worry about. We've known each other for months." She looked at the old guy sitting on the fountain, the one who had threatened Shane with a gun the night at the bar. "You were there at our first meeting, Uncle Jack. It was love at first sight and we've been seeing each other ever since." She leaned on Shane and sent him a loving smile.

Brother Buck spoke. "Wait a second, you're telling me that you, my hellion sister, went and fell in love with a preacher?" He started laughing so hard he had to sit down on the fountain next to Uncle Jack.

The older brother, Stetson, didn't look as amused. "That's enough, Buck. This isn't funny." He turned to Delaney. "You have some explaining to do, Del." He glanced at Kitty Carson. "In private."

Kitty took the hint and backed toward the break in the hedge. "I'll just get back to the party." And no doubt spread the news about what Reverend Ransom had been doing in the garden with Delaney Kingman. Shane couldn't let her do that.

"Wait, Ms. Carson," he said as he untangled his hand from Delaney. "I need to make something clear first. I'm not Chance Ransom. I'm his twin brother, Shane."

Kitty wagged her finger at him. "Now don't start that again. I know you're the man I was just talking to at the ball."

Rather than try to explain, Shane pulled out his cellphone that had a row of incoming texts from Chance asking him where he was. He fired off a text telling him and then returned his attention to the Kingmans. "Chance had planned to introduce me to everyone tonight at the ball, but I was late and I couldn't find him. He should be here any minute."

"Does your brother know about your engagement to my sister?" Stetson asked.

Shane hesitated. He didn't want to make Delaney out as a liar in front of her entire family. Especially when she'd only lied so her brothers wouldn't punch him out.

"I wouldn't say we're actually engaged."

The dark-haired man who Shane recognized from the night at Nasty Jack's stepped forward. From the intense look on his face, Shane figured he was more to Delaney than just the town bartender. "Exactly what would you say? Why does my sister think you're engaged and you don't? Have you been playing her?"

"Of course not." Delaney jumped in. "Just calm down, Wolfe. We aren't exactly engaged because . . . Shane and I haven't been able to go shopping for the ring yet. He wanted me to pick it out."

As much as he didn't want to embarrass Delaney, this farce was getting way out of hand. "That's not the reason. We're not, nor have we ever been—"

"Shane!" Chance's voice cut him off. A few seconds later, his brother appeared. Shane knew everyone thought he and his brother looked identical. But when he looked at Chance, he didn't see the similarities as much as the differences.

Chance was always groomed to perfection. His hair was cut short and styled and his face clean shaven. He always wore his shirts heavily starched and his jeans creased. Unlike Shane who hadn't had a haircut in a good six months or shaved in a good three days. He didn't iron his western shirts and jeans. He was lucky if he found a shirt and pair of jeans that were clean.

But other people only saw the similarities.

Kitty let out a startled gasp. "Well, I'll be. It's just like seein' double." She hustled over to Chance. "Thank goodness you're here, Reverend Ransom. There has been a big mix-up. It all started when I stepped outside to get away from that witch Hester Malone's evil eye—you really need to do something about that woman. Anyway, I was walking through the garden when that mean billy goat started chasing me." She glanced at the goat that had gone back to munching on the roses in the corner of the garden. "He chased me right here where I ran into your twin brother." She swatted Chance on the arm. "Shame on you for not telling me you had a brother who looks identical to you." She swatted him again. "And shame on you for not telling anyone he was engaged to our sweet little Delaney."

Chance's eyes widened, and he glanced over at Shane. "Engaged?"

Kitty waggled a finger between Shane and Delaney. "It looks like you two have been keeping secrets from everyone." She looked back at Chance. "It's lucky for you Delaney told the truth or you might be looking for another job. I was about to call a special meeting of the church board. We can't have a pastor taking liberties with our sweet little Del." She flashed a bucktoothed smile at Shane and Delaney. "But you can't fault two engaged lovebirds for doing a little cuddlin'."

"It's not up to you to fault anyone," Shane said.

"Two adult people don't have to be engaged to enjoy each other's company. And we're not—"

Delaney cut him off and completed his sentence. "Going to put up with people getting involved in our relationship. Which is why we wanted to keep our engagement a secret. I knew everyone would try to put their two cents' worth in. But Shane is right. We are two adults who don't need anyone's permission to cuddle in a garden." She walked over and picked up his hat, then grabbed her bra off the fountain. She glanced around, no doubt looking for her panties, but those were in Shane's back pocket. Something he wasn't about to confess in front of her angry brothers.

When she couldn't find her panties, she walked back over, plopped Shane's hat on his head, and took his hand. "Now if you'll excuse us, I'd like to enjoy the ball with my fiancé before it's over." She looked at the goat. "Come on, Karl. You're done enough damage to those roses."

The goat stopping munching and ambled toward the woman, but Shane wasn't an animal to be ordered around. When she tried to tug him toward the opening in the hedge, he stood his ground . . . until she turned pleading blue eyes on him. Then just like the goat, he allowed her to lead him out of the garden.

He expected her to take him to the castle. Instead, she took him in the opposite direction, past a bunkhouse and huge stables to a big red barn. Two dogs raced out. They froze when they saw Shane and started to growl. Delaney quickly got after them.

"Shame on you, Dex and Raleigh. Is that any way to treat a guest?"

The dogs stopped growling and ran over to greet Delaney, who showered them with head rubs and ear scratches. They followed her inside the barn just like the goat and Shane. Once there, she turned on the lights and guided the goat into a stall with one final pat on the butt.

"Sleep tight, Karl. No more night excursions." She secured the latch.

Upon hearing her voice, the animals in the other stalls mooed and squealed and baaed and mehhed until she went by each stall to greet them.

When she returned to Shane, he couldn't help asking. "Who are you? Farmyard Doctor Dolittle?"

Delaney laughed as she crouched down to pet the calico cat rubbing against her legs. "I just get along with animals."

"Obviously." He crossed his arms. "Just not with your family."

She sent him a startled look. "I get along with my family."

"Then why did you lie to them?"

"I lied for your brother. I didn't want him getting fired."

"Why would Chance get fired when Kitty now knows that I was the one kissing you?"

Her eyebrows arched. "Kissing? I think she caught us doing a little more than kissing. I bet I still have your handprint on my butt."

The memory of her sweet ass filling his hand

had him hardening beneath his fly. Or maybe it wasn't the memory as much as the way she was looking at him. Like she was remembering too.

In the overhead lights, he got his first real look at her. He had thought she looked like a siren when he'd first seen her in the maze garden. But it was nothing compared to how she looked now. Her hair was wild from his fingers and her lips were swollen from his kisses and along the edge of her neckline was a little love bite. The desire to kiss it better—or maybe give her another one—was so strong he had to turn away.

"It doesn't matter what Kitty caught us doing," he said. "As I said, we're adults. What we do or don't do is no one's business but our own."

She laughed. "I guess you didn't grow up in a small town."

"No. I grew up in Dallas."

"Then you don't know how a small town works. It doesn't matter if you're a kid or an adult, whatever you do in a small town is everyone's business. What happened in the garden is going to be spread all over Cursed by morning. Since most of the townsfolk are here, probably sooner than that."

He turned back around to find her sitting on a bale of hay with her dress hiked up to her knees . . . looking even sexier if that was possible.

"I get it," he said. "You have to live here and you're worried about your reputation. But I'm not willing to go along with this entire engagement farce just because of some small-town gossip. The thought that Kitty would talk to the church board and have my brother fired just because she caught us having a little fun is ludicrous."

She held out her hands. "Welcome to small-town life, where blood is thicker than water and families are judged as a whole not as individuals. If you have an alcoholic in the family, you can't take a drink without the town thinking you need to go to rehab. If your sister is promiscuous, you can't date a boy without people whispering about what you did in the back seat of his truck. If your brother is caught getting frisky with a woman he just met, everyone will think that womanizing runs in your family. If your brother was a long-time member of the community, the gossip would just be gossip. But he's new to Cursed. And new folks are judged even harsher. Pastors of the church, even more so."

He stared at her as the truth of her words sank in. He ran a hand through his hair before he sighed. "This could've been avoided if you had told me who you were."

"Or if you told me who you were. There's no way I would've done anything with the new preacher's family. So I think we're both at fault here."

Since she was right, he turned and walked a few steps away before he looked back at her. "How long? How long do we have to keep this farce up before we can break it off and go our separate ways?"

"Just until folks believe we're actually engaged. A couple weeks at most. I'll be the one to break it off so the town won't take it out on you. I'll just say I wasn't ready to get married—which they'll believe because everyone in town thinks I'm young and impulsive."

"How old are you?"

She grinned. "Worried I'm underage?"

"No. You have to be at least twenty-one to get in a bar."

"Not if your uncle owns it."

Fear punched him hard in the gut. But before he could pass out, she laughed.

"Don't panic. I'm only kidding. I'm twenty-five."

His shoulders sagged in relief and he joined her on the bales of hay. "Smartass."

She bumped his shoulder with hers. "It runs in my family."

"It looks like more badasses run in your family than smartasses. You have four brothers?"

"Three. The other one is my brother-in-law. Although Gage is even more of a badass. He's an ex-marine."

"Great." He blew out his breath and reached down to pet the cat circling Delaney's legs. "So where do we go from here? I have an apartment in Dallas and a business. If I'm not here, how can we prove to the town we're engaged?"

"All you need to do is visit me on the weekends and bring me gaudy bouquets of flowers and maybe text me a few sappy poems I can show people."

"So I take it you don't like flowers and poems?"

"I'd rather get dark chocolate or a horse."

He laughed. "Dark chocolate it is. I can't afford

a horse. Especially the kind you're used to."

She shrugged. "I'm not snobby about horses. And if you can't afford chocolate, that's fine too. What do you do?"

"I'm a software engineer. I do freelance app developing for companies. And I hope to run my own software development company one day." And make a fortune while he was at it.

"So you're a computer geek."

He wasn't really a computer geek. Geeks were passionate about everything to do with technology. He had only chosen the field because it seemed like the easiest way to make money. He was through with being poor. But he kept that information to himself.

"Yeah, I'm a geek. I'm certainly not a cowboy." He glanced around. "This is the first time I've been in a barn. Or even on a ranch."

She studied him for a long moment before she burst out laughing. He might have taken offense to being laughed at if she hadn't had the kind of laughter that was contagious. The kind that took over her entire body causing her to fall against him as she released breathy giggles that were accompanied by little snorts.

He couldn't help chuckling as he placed an arm around her to keep her from falling off the hay bale. "So I guess that's funny."

She shook her head against his shoulder and continued to laugh. Finally, her laughter slowed to a few giggles and she took a deep, quivery breath before she lifted her dancing blue eyes to him. "It's not the fact that you've never been on a ranch that's funny. It's the fact that I'm now engaged to a man who has never been on a ranch."

She started laughing again.

But Shane no longer saw the humor.

Chapter Four

With all the chaos of departing guests and cleaning caterers, Delaney was able to avoid her family and slip into her room without getting interrogated. But when she woke the following morning, she knew it was just a matter of time before her siblings started knocking at her door and wanting answers. So she got up, showered, and dressed, then headed downstairs to deal with the fallout of her impulsive behavior head on.

Claiming she and Shane were engaged *had* been impulsive. Once she'd found out he wasn't the new pastor, she should have confessed all. But something had held her back. It wasn't worry over the new pastor getting fired. Or her brothers roughing Shane up. Those two reasons played into it, but they weren't the main reason she'd come up with the engagement charade. The main reason had to do with what Shane had done to her in the garden. Not just the way he'd kissed her and caressed her and given her an amazing orgasm. But the way he'd let her set the pace and never pushed her to do anything she hadn't been ready to do.

He was the perfect gentleman lover.

Her perfect gentleman lover.

She knew if she confessed the truth to her brothers, they would make sure Shane didn't come knocking at her door again. She just couldn't have that. Not when Shane had shown her a glimpse of paradise. She wanted more than a glimpse. She wanted him to take her on a sexual guided tour and teach her everything she didn't know. If that meant she had to stretch the truth about his brother getting fired, so be it.

Not that it couldn't happen. The townsfolk were judgey. She just doubted that her sister, Adeline, or her sisters-in-law, Gretchen and Lily, or even her friend, Mystic Malone, would stand still for the town firing the new pastor. It wasn't like Delaney's little white lie would cause Shane any harm. All he had to sacrifice were a few weekends of being her sex ed teacher and she intended to make them as enjoyable for him as they were for her. What man would get upset about that?

Now that Shane was her fiancé, her brothers would no longer be standing guard over her virginity. Something she planned to lose at Shane's earliest convenience. In fact, maybe even today. Although locale was going to pose a problem. Her brothers might not stand guard over her, but they weren't about to let her waltz him up to her bedroom. Even if they did, she doubted Shane would go. He seemed to be a little skittish around her since their engagement. She hadn't even been able to get a kiss from him before he'd left last night.

But she would figure out a perfect place for their sex lair. She had always been resourceful.

"Just what are you scheming, little girl?"

Delaney pulled out of her thoughts as she stepped into the kitchen. She had expected to find her entire family sitting at the table eating breakfast, but only Uncle Jack and Potts, the family cook, were there. Since Uncle Jack had come to live with them, the two crusty old cowboys had become fast friends. Potts was a good fifteen years younger than Uncle Jack, but just as opinionated.

"She's always scheming something, this one," Potts said as he pulled out a chair for Delaney. "Engaged to a preacher's brother?" He shook his head. "Lord have mercy on us all."

Delaney took a seat. "The Lord doesn't need to have mercy. There's nothing wrong with me being engaged to a preacher's brother."

"I'm sure the preacher don't feel that way. I'm sure he was hopin' his brother would marry a good churchgoing woman. Not some wild cowgirl who hasn't shown her face in church in years."

"You should talk, Potts." She helped herself to some of Potts's French toast casserole. "When was the last time you went to church?"

"I'm not marryin' no preacher's brother."

"But if Miss Kitty has her way, you might be headed to church," Uncle Jack said with a smirk.

Delaney stared at Potts. "Miss Kitty?"

Potts's face flushed. "Kitty isn't interest in this

old cowboy. She's friendly with everyone."

Uncle Jack chuckled. "But she doesn't brighten up like a firefly when she's delivering the mail to me."

"'Cause you're an ornery old cuss. Miss Kitty isn't interested in gettin' me to the altar."

"You could be right about that. She could just be in lust." Uncle Jack glanced over at Delaney. "Like someone else we know."

Delaney froze with a forkful of ooey gooey French toast inches from her mouth. "What do you mean by that?"

Uncle Jack snorted. "There was only one thing I saw in your eyes the first time you looked at Shane . . . and it wasn't love. Which is why I followed you out to the bar parking lot. And considering what you two were caught doing in the garden last night, I don't think things have changed."

Damn. She hadn't realized her uncle was so observant.

"Well, shouldn't you have a healthy bit of lust for your fiancé?" she asked before she took the bite of French toast.

"There's a difference between lust with love and lust without. But I figure you'll learn that soon enough."

"If they wait to get married," Potts said as he poured her a cup of coffee. "If Delaney is in an all-fired hurry to get hitched like the rest of her family, they won't figure it out until the weddin' night."

"I'm in no hurry to get married." Delaney

continued to eat. "Both Shane and I want a long engagement. Especially since his home is in Dallas and my home is here." Potts and Uncle Jack turned to stare at her. "What? We can have a long-distance relationship. People do it all the time. Shane will come here on the weekends, and maybe some weekends I can go to Dallas to visit him."

"And when you get married?" Uncle Jack asked. "What then? I can't see you leaving this ranch."

None of her family ever saw her leaving the ranch. Delaney couldn't see it either. She loved the ranch as much as she loved her family. But . . . sometimes she did wonder what it would be like to have a small place where abused animals could find refuge. But it was a ridiculous dream. What kind of fool would want a small ranch when they owned a huge one? Throwing a coin in a fountain and wishing for it was pure nonsense.

"We'll work it out," she said. But it was obvious by the looks on their faces that neither Potts nor Uncle Jack believed her. It was a relief when the rest of her family arrived.

Usually on Sundays, everyone came down to breakfast in their pajamas or ranch clothes. But today, her family was all showered and wearing nice dresses and starched western shirts and jeans.

Even Gretchen and Wolfe. Delaney thought if anyone was going to sleep in, it would be a newlywed couple. Her brother and Gretchen's small wedding ceremony had been held right before the Cowboy Ball. Only now did Delaney think about how she had probably ruined their wedding day by being caught in the garden with Shane—and by her engagement announcement. But she would apologize to them later. Right now, she was wondering what was going on.

"Why are y'all dressed up?" she asked.

"We're going to church," Adeline said. "And so are you. Hurry and change clothes."

She took the last bite of her French toast. "No, thank you. I have about a zillion things to get done on the ranch today."

"They'll wait," Stetson said. "Since Pastor Ransom will soon be part of our family, we need to be there—not just to show him our support, but also to let the town know we support your and his brother's decision. In fact, it was decided that Pastor Ransom will be announcing your engagement at church today."

Delaney eyes widened. Lying to your family was one thing. Lying in church was something else entirely. She might not be a churchgoing Christian, but she believed in God . . . and in his wrath.

"Umm . . . maybe it would be better if we made the announcement to the town another time." Like never. "I'm sure Kitty has taken care of telling all the townsfolk."

"What's wrong, Delly Belly?" Buck asked with a mischievous twinkle in his eyes. "Getting cold feet already?"

Since there was no way to explain her hesitance without confessing her lie, she glared at her twin brother. "Not at all. I just think we should wait until Shane can be there too. He told me last night he was heading back to Dallas today."

"I'm sure he changed his mind," Stetson said. "Now get on something other than your work clothes and let's go."

It turned out that Shane *had* changed his mind—or had his mind changed for him by his brother—and was waiting outside of Holy Gospel with Chance when Delaney and her family arrived.

The Ransoms were identical twins, but it was easy to tell them apart. Not only because Chance wore a suit and tie and Shane wore faded jeans and a wrinkled western shirt, but also because Shane's hair was longer and his gaze more intense. That gaze zeroed in on Delaney as soon as she jumped down from Buck's green monster truck. She figured he was as happy about his brother announcing their engagement in church as she was.

But he didn't show it as he brushed a soft kiss on her cheek. "Good mornin'."

The simple greeting and gesture had her feeling shy and at a loss for words—two things she had never felt in her life. They had to be side effects of the great orgasm he'd given her. That was the only explanation for her feeling all flushed and speechless. She grew even more so when Shane took her hand and placed it in the crook of his arm. "We better find our pew."

"No need for that," Stetson said. "We have a family pew right up front. You can sit with us."

Shane hesitated for a second as if he wanted to

argue. Instead, he nodded. "Of course. Nothing like a front row seat." He held out a hand to her family. "After y'all." All the Kingmans headed into church—except for Buck. He chose to follow Delaney and Shane and sit right next to them.

"I don't believe we were properly introduced last night." Buck held out his hand to Shane. "I'm Buck Kingman."

Delaney finished the introduction. "My little brother and a royal pain in the butt."

"I'm not littler," Buck said. "I'm only younger. And just by a few minutes."

Shane glanced at her with surprise. "You're a twin?"

"Wait a second," Buck said. "Del didn't tell you?"

"It's not something I'm proud of," she hedged. "Now be quiet, the service is starting."

Chance Ransom was a good preacher. He was friendly and witty and had the entire congregation smiling after only a few minutes of his sermon. Shane smiled brighter than everyone. It was obvious he was more than a little proud of his brother. It was also obvious he had been to church a few times. He knew when to stand and when to bow his head and how to find the right hymn in the hymnal.

Not that he needed a hymnal. He knew the words by heart and sang them in a strong, deep voice that made Delaney feel overly warm. From the corner of her eye, she watched his firm lips form every word. She had never wanted to kiss someone so much in all her life.

Instead, she fanned herself with the Sunday program and mouthed the words like she knew what she was doing. When the singing was over, she sat down and noticed Uncle Jack watching her from farther down the pew. He arched an eyebrow as if he knew exactly the impure thoughts she'd been thinking. She scowled and quickly looked away.

When Chance finished the sermon and started making the announcements, Delaney's palms started to sweat and she couldn't keep from glancing up at the ceiling and wondering if it was strong enough to take a bolt of lightning without caving in.

Shane's low chuckle pulled her gaze to his smiling face. It wasn't the fake smile he'd been giving her for the benefit of their families and the townsfolk. This smile was real and warmed her even more than his singing had. He leaned in and whispered next to her ear.

"Worried?" He reached over and took her hand, linking her fingers in a secure grip as he glanced up at the ceiling. "It's okay. If we get struck, we'll go down together."

Strangely, his words made her feel better. Maybe because they made her feel like she wasn't alone. Shane might not like her plan, but he was willing to go along with it. As they stood to have their engagement recognized by the congregation, she no longer worried about God's wrath. With her fingers entwined with Shane's, she looked around at the smiling townsfolk and was consumed by a warm feeling of happiness and contentment.

Delaney Kingman finally had a steady boyfriend.

Chapter Five

SHANE HAD IMAGINED a lot of unlikely scenarios over the years. Like the fantasy he had as a kid where he'd start his own *Monster Garage* and trick out cars and motorcycles on a hit television show. Or the one he had as a teenager where he'd start a band and become an overnight sensation and get sex with hot groupies whenever he wanted. Or the one he still had where he'd make billions of dollars on a new app and buy a deserted island where he would surround himself with bikini models and eat nothing but porterhouse steaks, lobster, and Ding Dongs flown in on his private helicopter from the mainland.

But he had never imagined standing in church in front of an entire town while his brother announced his fake engagement. That scenario had never even entered his mind.

And yet, here he was.

He glanced up to see Chance watching him as intently as he'd been watching him since he'd gotten up that morning. Chance had always been able to read through Shane's lies. But hopefully Shane could continue to avoid telling his brother the truth until Delaney broke things off. If Chance knew the engagement was a farce, he would never go along with it.

Even if it meant he lost his job as pastor of Holy Gospel.

Shane couldn't let that happen. Chance needed a new start. He needed to put the last year behind him and find happiness again. Losing his wife, Lori, and their beloved grandmother in the same year had devastated Chance. Shane hadn't realized how much until his brother had quit his job as a pastor of a small church in Austin to stay holed up in his apartment.

Worried about Chance, Shane had started looking for new pastoring jobs for his brother. The name of Cursed had intrigued him, as did the story he found on the website about how Cursed got its name. According to the story, the first settlers had been beset by drought, dust storms, floods, tornados, pestilence, and everything else Mother Nature could throw at them. They weathered it all and built a town. Shane figured those were the kind of persevering folks his brother needed right now. Folks who would help Chance get through his loss and move on. So he had masqueraded as his brother and come to Cursed to check out the Holy Gospel church.

What Shane hadn't planned on was running into a sassy cowgirl.

When Chance agreed to come to Cursed for an interview with the church board and they hired him on the spot, Shane had stopped off at the only bar in town for a celebratory beer. If he had been happy with a beer, he wouldn't be standing in front of the townsfolk and God and lying through his teeth. But when he'd stepped into Nasty Jack's and spotted the pool tables at the back, his ego had him wanting to prove his prowess on the green felt. Instead, he'd lost. Badly. He would've left with only his bruised pride if Delaney hadn't hopped into his truck before he could even start it up. Once her lips landed on his, he didn't care about losing. All he'd cared about was getting more of the how woman who had fallen into his arms.

Even now, in the middle of church, he warred with the strong desire to pull Delaney into his arms and kiss her. Instead, he kept his gaze away from her soft lips and nodded as the townsfolk joyously applauded.

As they sat down, he went to release Delaney's hand, but she held tightly. Maybe she was still feeling nervous about their lie. Or maybe she just wanted to convince her family they were a couple in love. Whatever the reason, he didn't mind. Her hand fit nicely in his. After the service was over and they released hands to file out of the pew, he missed the connection and rested his hand on the small of her back until they were outside where the townsfolk were waiting to congratulate them.

Shane had hoped he could make a quick getaway after the service. He had a meeting first thing the following morning with an investor and he needed to get back to Dallas. Not that this meeting would go any better than the last three had gone. But he still couldn't lose hope that someone would be willing to invest in his idea for an app that he was sure would make him his first million—if not more. All he needed was financing to hire more software developers and pay for the marketing to launch it.

Now it looked like he would have to wait to head back to Dallas. Everyone seemed to be thrilled about their engagement and wanted to chat. The townsfolk seemed to adore Delaney and were extremely protective of her. He lost count of how many men shook his hand too firmly and issued a warning about taking care of their sweet, innocent little gal.

Did they even know Delaney? Shane didn't know her well, but he knew her well enough to know she didn't need anyone taking care of her. As for being sweet and innocent, innocent women didn't hop into strangers' trucks and kiss them senseless . . . or allow them to take the kind of liberties Shane had taken in the garden.

Not that he was complaining. He liked women who knew what they wanted and were up for a little sexual adventure. But he couldn't understand why the townsfolk kept referring to her as some sheltered princess who needed to be handled with care.

"So Del found her mystery man."

He turned to see a pretty dark-haired woman standing there. He had met her when he'd been pretending to be Chance, but he couldn't remember her name. All he knew was that she was somehow related to Hester Malone. Which made him more than a little leery.

"I'm not much of a mystery," he said.

She tipped her head. "I wouldn't agree. It's a mystery to me why a man would masquerade as his brother. My grandmother was right. You weren't a preacher."

He glanced around to see if anyone was listening, but most of the people were gathered around Delaney waiting to talk with her. He looked back at Mystic. "I hope you'll keep that between us. My brother was going through a difficult time and needed to get back to preaching. So I took it upon myself to do a little job searching. I didn't mean any harm. I just wanted to make sure Chance would be happy here."

Her eyebrows lifted. "And you thought he would be even after you saw my grandmother and Kitty bickering?" She held out a hand. "Mystic Malone."

His shoulders relaxed, and he took her hand. "Shane Ransom. Your grandmother and Kitty don't get along, do they? I thought they were going to go after each other last night at the Cowboy Ball."

"I figure they'll have it out one day, and hopefully it will clear the air and allow them to get along."

He squinted. "You really think so?"

She laughed. "Probably not." She hesitated and studied him with her unusual violet eyes. "So how did it happen? How did Delaney's mystery cowboy suddenly become her fiancé?"

"How does love ever happen?" he hedged. "It just does."

Again she studied him. But this time, it left him feeling like he did when her grandmother stared at him. Like she was reading all his thoughts. She finally pulled her gaze from him and looked at Delaney who was talking with Kitty Carson. Or not talking as much as listening as Kitty chatted nonstop. When Mystic returned her attention to him, her eyes held concern.

"Are you sure you two are ready for marriage?"

Once again, he dodged the question with a question. "Is anyone ever ready for marriage? It's a big step, but sometimes you just need to jump."

That didn't seem to appease Mystic. She looked even more concerned. "I don't think jumping into marriage is a good idea. Both my grandmother and mother did and it didn't turn out well for either one. Speaking of my grandmother, I'm going to go get her. I'm sure Hessy will want to congratulate you too."

But Shane wasn't about to wait around for the town clairvoyant. As soon as Mystic left to get her grandmother, he headed over to Delaney and Kitty.

"Can I steal my fiancée away for a few seconds, Ms. Carson?" Before Kitty could answer, he drew Delaney away from the crowd and around the side of the church.

"What's going on?" Delaney asked.

"Mystic knows something is up. She went to get her grandmother to congratulate me . . . or more likely try to look into my brain."

"Holy crap! We need to get out of here."

"My thoughts exactly." He opened the passenger door of his truck and helped her in before he hurried around to the driver's side. On the way out of the parking lot, he saw Hester and Mystic standing in front of the church glancing around and he felt a little foolish for being so concerned.

"She can't really read minds, can she?"

"I don't know about mind reading, but I do know she can see the future. When I asked her if I'd ever see you again, she knew you'd come back to town and we'd get together. I just didn't realize how together we were going to get."

He glanced over at her. "You went to Hester to find out if you'd ever see me again?"

Her cheeks grew pink, but she didn't look away. "What can I say? You're a good kisser."

The compliment had him smiling. "I couldn't forget our kiss either."

Her cheeks grew pinker. "I bet you say that to all the girls."

He returned his attention to the road. "Actually, I haven't dated that much lately. I've been too busy with work. I shouldn't have even stayed for church this morning, but my brother was pretty adamant about announcing our engagement."

"So was mine. Of course, Stetson is always adamant about what he wants."

"He does seem like a man who is used to being in charge."

"Rightfully so. He's worked his butt off to make the ranch what it is today. But so have . . ." She let the sentence drift off. "It doesn't matter. It is what it is."

He glanced at her and finished her sentence.

"But so have you and you're tired of being bossed around."

She looked at him and lifted her eyebrows. "So now you're a mind reader?"

He laughed. "No. It's a typical little sibling complaint. I'm the oldest by a few minutes. But those few minutes make a big difference in the family dynamic. I've always felt like I need to be the one who watches out for Chance. And I meddle a little more in his life than I probably should. But I just want what's best for him. I'm sure Stetson feels the same."

"But how do you know what's best for someone? Shouldn't they be the ones to make those decisions?"

She had a good point.

"You're right, but I guess it's hard for older siblings to let go of their responsibility. Have you tried letting Stetson know how you feel?"

"Yes, but me complaining about wanting a say in how the ranch is run goes in one ear and out the other."

"Maybe you need to be more specific. What would you change if you had the chance? And how is that change going to impact the ranch and make more profit?"

She sighed. "That's just it. It won't make more profit for the ranch. It will only cost money."

"Okay, now I'm intrigued. What do you want to do?"

She shook her head. "It's silly."

"Come on. 'Fess up. You can't get any sillier than a fake engagement."

"You have a point." She hesitated. "I want to use a section of the ranch for a refuge for abused and neglected animals."

After seeing how she connected with animals, he wasn't surprised. "That's not silly. It's smart. It might not be profitable, but it's charitable. And good companies are both. They make money, but they also give some of that money back to the community. It's good business."

"We already give a lot of money back to our community. The Kingman Ranch donates to the schools, Holy Gospel, and all the town fundraisers. Fundraisers my sister Adeline usually spearheads, along with the Cursed Ladies' Auxiliary Club. So it's not like we're not charitable. It's just that . . ."

"This is something you feel passionate about. So talk to Stetson."

She shook her head. "I don't want to cause my brother any grief. I owe him and Adeline more than I could ever repay. They pretty much raised me, Buck, and Wolfe after our mother passed away." He wanted to ask more questions about her mother . . . and the father she hadn't mentioned, but she abruptly ended the conversation. "And what about you? What are you passionate about?"

He thought about lying and then answered honestly. "Making money."

"And have you made a lot?"

"Not yet, but I'm working on it. My goal is to make my first million by the time I'm twenty-eight."

"Is that why you want to start your own company? To be a millionaire?"

"I'm thinking more billionaire." He glanced over at her. "Are you having second thoughts about marrying a money-hungry computer geek?"

She scooted across the bench seat and placed a hand on his thigh. Her gaze lowered to his mouth and her top teeth slid over the plump flesh of her bottom lip. "Not yet."

A punch of desire hit him in the gut and he almost missed the turnoff to the Kingman Ranch. He took it going a little fast and the back tires of his truck fishtailed before he could straighten out. When he glanced at Delaney, she was looking at him like he was a tempting dessert she couldn't wait to dive into.

And why not let her dive? If he was stuck in a fake engagement, he might as well enjoy the benefits. He had plenty of time to get back to Dallas.

He pulled off onto a dirt road that led to a copse of mesquite and oak trees. Once in their shade, he parked and turned to her.

She smiled seductively as she slid her hand closer to his growing erection. "Whatcha doin', cowboy? Or I guess I can't call you a cowboy if you can't even ride."

"Oh, I can ride." He pulled her onto his lap. "But maybe you'd like to do the riding today."

There was a flicker of uncertainty in her eyes that surprised him. He didn't take Delaney for a missionary-type girl. But he must've imagined her apprehension because a second later she looped her arms around his neck and smiled.

"With pleasure." She kissed him.

Delaney's kisses were a sweet mixture of soft lips and wicked tongue. She kissed like she played pool. With total focus. It didn't take long for Shane to have a hard-on that could break a rack of pool balls. Especially when she started wiggling her butt against him. He was thankful for the jean skirt she wore. He had waited a long time for this. He didn't want to wait a second more.

He slid his hand beneath her skirt and slipped her panties down to her knees before he delved back under her skirt. Wet heat welcomed him. He knew if he didn't get inside that heat soon he would go insane. But when he went to move her off his lap so he could undo his fly, she held tight.

"I want you," she whispered against his lips.

"I want you too, baby. But I need to get my pants down first."

She drew back and looked a little embarrassed. "Oh. Of course." She slid off his lap.

He quickly unbuttoned and unzipped his jeans. He was just about to push them down when the sound of an approaching vehicle had him glancing out the back window.

The same green monster truck Delaney had arrived at church in was barreling toward them.

Damned if they weren't going to be interrupted again.

Chapter Six

With a cussed oath, Shane zipped and buttoned his jeans.

"What's wrong?" Delaney asked with desire-filled eyes that had him leaning over to give her another kiss.

"We have company." He rolled down his window as Buck pulled up next to his truck.

While he and Chance looked identical, Buck and Delaney only had a few similarities. They both had the same sky blue eyes and the same stubborn chins. But Buck looked more like Adeline with his platinum-blond hair and soft features while Delaney looked more like Wolfe with her black hair and distinct features.

"Hey, y'all," Buck said with a wide grin. There was something contagious about his smile and Shane couldn't help smiling back.

Delaney didn't feel the same. She leaned over Shane and glared at her brother. "Go home, Buck. We don't want company."

"If you didn't want company you shouldn't have parked in clear sight of the road." He had a good point. Shane mentally chastised himself for not parking behind the trees instead of in front of them.

"So what do you want, Buck?" Delaney asked. "And make it quick."

"Stetson invited Shane's brother over for lunch so we can celebrate y'all's engagement as one big happy family."

"Well, tell Stetson we'll be there when we get—"

Shane placed a hand on Delaney's knee and stopped her. "I think I've ticked your brothers off enough." He looked at Buck. "We'll follow you back."

When Buck pulled away, Delaney grumbled. "Am I ever going to get you alone?"

Shane laughed as he followed Buck. "It's okay. We'll have plenty of time to finish what we started when I come back next weekend." In fact, he was thinking that maybe he'd come back a little sooner. Although, with her family, he was starting to wonder if he'd ever get to enjoy his fake engagement.

Lunch with all the Kingmans certainly wasn't enjoyable. It was awkward and uncomfortable. Everyone watched Shane like he was a bug under a magnifying glass. Chance did too. It was like he was waiting for Shane to laugh and say it was just a joke. All the staring seemed to make Delaney nervous and she chattered nonstop about her goats.

It was a huge relief when lunch was over.

Or so Shane thought.

Before he could make his excuses and head

back to Dallas, Stetson asked to talk to him in his study. The room had rich, dark paneling and wide planked floors partially covered by a thick area rug. On one wall was a floor-to-ceiling bookcase. On the other was a fireplace with a collection of animal antlers above it.

Stetson sat down behind the massive desk in front of the window and pointed to a chair. "Please sit down, Shane." He glanced at Delaney, who had followed Shane into the study. "Close the door on your way out, Del."

"I'm not leaving." Delaney crossed her arms and stood her ground. "Not when you've chased off every one of my potential boyfriends."

Stetson returned his attention to Shane. "If they chase off easily, they aren't worth having." The message came in loud and clear.

Shane smiled at Delaney. "I'm not going anywhere. I failed miserably at track and field."

She laughed, but her eyes still held doubt. Shane had to wonder exactly how many boyfriends her brothers had run off. She finally released a sigh and nodded. "Fine. But I lettered in track and field. So if you do decide to run off, know that I'll catch you."

He grinned at the thought of Delaney chasing him down. He didn't doubt for a second that she could do it. "Duly noted."

After sending a narrow-eyed look at her brother, she turned and walked out of the room, closing the door behind her. When she was gone, Shane took a chair and hooked his hat on his knee while Stetson sat down behind the desk.

The clock on the wall ticked off the time while Shane waited for the interrogation to begin. It didn't take long.

"So you're a software developer."

"I guess Delaney told you."

Stetson shook his head. "I called my private investigator and had him do a background check. We're all a little stunned over your and Delaney's engagement. She's always been impulsive, but marriage wasn't high on her list of things to do. Now suddenly she wants to get married to a man none of us know. It would be stupid not to investigate you. Especially when there are plenty of men who would see marrying a Kingman as an opportunity to better their lot in life. And I'm going to be straight with you. You won't marry Delaney without first signing a prenup. Not one percent of this ranch will ever be owned by anyone who doesn't carry Kingman blood."

"Understood. I don't want your ranch or your money."

Stetson's eyes narrowed. "Hmm?" He glanced at the laptop screen in front of him. "It looks like you're interested in money to me. Otherwise why are you meeting with investors?"

Whoever Stetson had gotten to investigate him was good. Shane would give him that. "Are you telling me that you've never borrowed money for your business?"

"And what business is that, Shane? I would think you'd make enough being a software developer."

"I don't want to develop software for other

people. I want to start my own company developing software applications designed to run on mobile devices. Right now, I'm working on an application that helps people take care of the elderly members of their family. It keeps track of doctor's appointments and medications. Alerts them of possible side effects when new medications are added. Doctors can download patient notes to it. I'm hoping to set it up so it will offer direct links to all elderly services in the area—homecare, shuttle services, grocery and meal delivery."

Stetson studied him for a long moment with his fingers steepled against his chin before he lowered them and nodded. "How did you come up with this idea?"

"My grandmother needed help as she got older and I was completely in the dark about how much help she needed. It was only after she was put in the hospital that Chance and I found out she hadn't been making her doctor's appointments because she was scared of driving." Something Shane still blamed himself for. He should have been taking her to her doctor's appointments and keeping track of her medicine. He'd been so busy with his dream of becoming wealthy—a dream that included buying his grandmother a house and making her life easier—that he hadn't realized she needed his help. In the present. Not in the future.

"I'm sorry she passed," Stetson said. "That must have been hard. Especially since she raised you and your brother."

Shane thought Stetson would bring up his parents. But he seemed smart enough to know that was a sensitive subject and moved away from questions about Shane's family to questions about his college years and the freelance work he now did. When Shane had pretty much spilled his entire life story, Stetson sat back in his chair and asked the one question Shane had been dreading.

"So why my sister?"

Shane hedged. "She's an amazing pool player for one. She fleeced me for every dime I had in my pocket."

Stetson laughed. "You should play poker with her. The ranch hands have learned to steer clear of any game that Delaney's playing in." His smile faded. "But seriously, why do you want to marry her? Especially when you don't seem to have a lot in common with her. You grew up in a big city and she grew up in the country. You spend most of your time on a computer and she spends most of her time with horses. You live in an apartment in downtown Dallas and she lives on a ranch. How do you think this marriage is going to work?"

He knew what Stetson wanted was for him to confess his undying love. But he couldn't baldfaced lie to the man. So he hedged. "Opposites attract. I'm sure there are a lot of married couples out there that didn't have a lot in common when they first got married. But they still made it work." Just not any married couples in his family. His grandparents on both sides had divorced. And his parents hadn't married. Maybe if his father hadn't died of a drug overdose, they would have. Or maybe not.

"And there are a lot more marriages that don't work," Stetson said, as if reading his mind.

Shane tried to ease his mind. "It's not like we're getting married right away. We have plenty of time to see if we're truly compatible."

"Plenty of time? How do you figure when you'll be living in Dallas and she's living here?"

"I plan on coming back to visit as often as I can." After their steamy kisses in the truck, he had started thinking about heading back to Cursed as soon as his meeting with the investor Dan Fuller was finished. But that was just his libido talking. He didn't need to let a woman get in his head and keep him from his goal. He needed to stay focused. The weekend was soon enough to make the trip back.

But it seemed Stetson had other ideas.

"I don't think a few weekends here and there is enough time for you and Delaney to see if you're truly compatible. Lily and I had known each other for years before we got married." Stetson hesitated. "Which is why I'd like you to move to the ranch."

Shane stared at him. "Excuse me?" He shook his head. "I'm sorry, but that's not possible."

"Why? I assume you can work anywhere your computer is."

"Yes, but I'd prefer to have my own work space."

"We have a large guest room with a desk I'm sure will work nicely for all your needs." His eyes drilled into Shane. "And you'll get to be with your fiancée. Why wouldn't a man who is in love want that?"

Shane was backed in a corner and Stetson knew it. Shane could either confess all or take Stetson up on the offer. And what would it hurt if he came to live on the ranch for a few weeks? It might even help to explain why he and Delaney broke up. Living together in the same household would make them realize they weren't well suited—something Stetson already seemed to think.

Smart man.

Still, Shane hated to be manipulated.

"I'll think about it," he said as he got to his feet. "Now I better head back to Dallas." He held out his hand. "Thank you for lunch, Stetson."

Stetson stood and took his hand. "I hope to see you soon, Shane."

After Shane left the office, he found Delaney standing in the foyer. She had changed out of the shirt and jean skirt she'd worn to church and was now wearing a T-shirt and worn jeans with her cowboy boots. The boots were newer and he knew exactly why she'd had to buy a new pair. She'd left one of her boots in his truck on the night they first met. The thought had him smiling.

She answered his smile with one of her own. "It looks like you didn't run for the hills."

"Nope."

"Good." She hooked her arm through his as they walked out the front door to his truck. "Did you pass the Stet Test?"

"I'm not sure I passed. I don't think he's completely bought our little charade. He invited me to stay here."

She turned to him. "Here? At the ranch?"

"That's what he said. He wants us to get to know each other better."

A seductive smile tipped up the corners of Delaney's mouth. She stepped closer and ran a finger along the open collar of his shirt. It was insane how the slightest brush of a single digit could fill his body with such an overwhelming wave of desire.

Stetson was right. They didn't have much in common. But what they did have was this unexplainable heat. From the moment she'd kissed him, he'd felt like a lit fuse. Delaney seemed to feel it too. Her eyes glittered with passion as she spoke in a low, sexy whisper.

"Well, I do like the thought of getting to know you better."

She looped her arms around his neck and kissed him.

That was all it took for Shane to make his decision.

He was moving into a castle.

Chapter Seven

Delaney spent most of the following morning looking for Karl. The goat had gone missing again. No matter what kind of latches she used on the barn stalls or pasture gates, the ornery animal figured them out. She looked everywhere. Including the castle. Karl had been known to let himself in the back door and try to pilfer Potts's pantry. But Potts hadn't seen the goat. Neither had Uncle Jack, who was sitting at the kitchen table playing dominos with Potts.

Thinking the goat might've made his way back into the garden to munch on the roses—the darn goat loved roses—Delaney stopped by there on her way back to the stables. She didn't find Karl, but she did find her sister and two sisters-in-law. Adeline, Lily, and Gretchen were sitting at the table just outside the garden cottage having what looked like a tea party. Since Delaney had successfully avoided talking to her sister about her engagement to Shane, she tried to duck behind some lilac bushes before they spotted her. Unfortunately, Adeline had always had eyes in the back of her head.

"Del!"

Delaney froze and turned toward the table. "Hey, y'all. I didn't see you sitting there. You haven't seen Karl, have you? The ornery goat got out again."

"Have you checked Buck's room?" Gretchen said. "He seems to love to munch on Buck's straw cowboy hats."

"Good idea, Gretch. I'll go check."

Adeline waved a hand. "You can check later. Come join us."

"I really need to find Karl before he does some damage and Buck starts yelling."

Adeline tipped her head and gave Delaney the disappointed look she'd perfected. Delaney hated to disappoint Addie. She sighed and moved down the garden path to the table. "I guess I can spare a few minutes." She helped herself to one of the warm scones piled high on a plate in the center of the table before she sat down in a chair. She took a bite and waited for the conversation to continue, but all eyes were now on her.

She swallowed. "Okay, I get it. You have a lot of questions. So go ahead. Shoot."

"Why didn't you say a word about falling in love?" Adeline said. "I'm your sister."

Actually, Adeline was more like her mother. Delaney and Buck had only been four when their mother had passed away. Growing up, it had been Addie they had run to for hugs and Band-Aids when they fell and scraped a knee. Addie who held their hands when they crossed a street and tucked them in at night. While Stetson had been the stern father figure who protected them, provided for them, and told them stories about their mother.

Delaney had to admit she felt pretty bad lying to them. All her life, she had worked hard to make Adeline and Stetson proud. But sometimes you just had to do something for yourself.

And Shane Ransom was something she wanted for herself.

If a little white lie would keep Shane here for a few weeks for her to enjoy, she didn't see anything wrong with that. It wasn't like they were actually going to get married.

"I didn't say anything to you, Addie, because you're just as protective as our brothers. You would've wanted to know all about Shane. If you didn't think he was right for me, you would've figured out some way to end it."

"Because you're my baby sister and I want what's best for you."

"Shane is what's best for me." It wasn't a lie. Every time she kissed him, she felt things she had never felt before. She wasn't stupid. She knew it was only lust. But if lust could make you feel invincible, then she wanted more of it.

Everyone thought she was so confident and strong. But the truth was that all her bragging and the constant need to prove herself came from a feeling that she wasn't good enough—that she would never be good enough. But when Shane kissed her. She felt different. She didn't feel like she was lacking. She felt like she was more than enough. She wasn't ready to give that feeling up.

Not even for her family.

But she didn't want them worrying either.

"It's okay, Addie," she said. "I'm a big girl. I can handle myself."

"Of course you can," Lily said. "Now tell us how you two fell in love."

Delaney took a bite of scone. "Well, there's not that much to tell. I met him at Nasty Jack's and it was pretty much love at first sight." Or more like lust at first sight. Shane had bent over the pool table to take a shot and she had gotten one look at his nice butt and decided he was the cowboy for her. Except he wasn't a cowboy. He was a computer geek who probably didn't even know how to ride a horse. God certainly had a sense of humor.

As she continued her story, she discovered she didn't have to fabricate much. "After Uncle Jack ran him off, I couldn't stop thinking about Shane. So I went to Hester to see if she could help me find him. She couldn't see where he was, but she told me he would return to Curse. And he did. One day, we ran into each other in town and we've been seeing each other ever since."

"You certainly look in love," Gretchen said. "You two couldn't keep your eyes off each other in church yesterday." She paused. "But you still need to be sure before you head to the altar. You don't want to end up like my mama." Gretchen's mama had been married more times than Delaney could keep track of.

"No worries there," Delaney said. "Unlike my siblings, I'm in no rush to tie the knot."

But she was in a rush to get Shane into bed. Every time things started to heat up between them, someone showed up and interrupted them. Her search for a sex lair wasn't going well. Lily and Stetson lived in the garden cottage. Tab, the stable manager, slept in the room at the back of the stables. The barn wasn't private enough and hay was damned itchy. And the bunkhouse was filled with rowdy cowboys.

Of course, now that Shane was moving into the castle for the next few weeks, it would be easy to sneak into each other's rooms at night. But having sex with her siblings right next door made her feel a little weird. It would be much better if she could find a place away from the house. A spot all their own to do whatever wicked things they wanted to.

Just the thought of doing wicked things with Shane had a rush of heat filling her body. She had just reached for a napkin to use as a fan when Mystic Malone came down the garden path. Mystic had gone to school with Buck and Delaney. While she was closest to Buck, she was Delaney's friend too.

"Hey, y'all," she said. "You having yourselves a little tea party? That was some Cowboy Ball, wasn't it? One Kingman gets married . . ." Mystic glanced at Delaney. "And one gets engaged."

"It was an exciting evening," Adeline said. "Come join us, Mystic. Lily made her famous scones with lemon curd."

"Thank you, but Monday is the one day I can clean the salon and get my accounting done without customers. So I need to get back."

"You drove all the way out here to see Buck for a few minutes?" Delaney asked. "Why didn't you just call?"

"Actually, I wanted to talk to you, Del." Mystic hesitated. "In private."

Delaney figured she knew what the private matter was about. Shane. But being interrogated by Mystic was better than being interrogated by her sister and sisters-in-law. She polished off the scone and got up. "Come on then. You can follow me to Buck's room to look for Karl."

Karl wasn't in Buck's room. After checking the closet to see if he was munching on Buck's hat, Delaney flopped down on the bed and tucked her hands behind her head.

"Okay, so what questions do you have about Shane?"

Mystic sat down on the edge of the bed. "I don't have any questions. I came here to tell you that Shane doesn't love you."

Delaney sat up. "What?"

Mystic released her breath in a long sigh. "What I'm about to tell you, you have to promise not to tell another soul. I wouldn't even be telling you if it wasn't a desperate situation. I couldn't live with myself if I let you marry a man who didn't love you the way you deserve to be loved."

"And how do you know Shane doesn't love me?"

"That's the part you have to swear not to tell anyone else. Not even Buck."

Since she and Buck had never been the type of

twins who share secrets, Delaney nodded. "Okay. I swear I won't tell anyone. Not even Buck. But I thought you and Buck shared everything."

"Not this." Mystic hesitated a long moment before she spoke. "You know how I told everyone that I don't have my grandmother's gift for seeing the future?"

Delaney's eyes widened. "You can see the future?"

"Not exactly. I can't see the future, but I can read people's emotions."

"That's not that difficult to do, Mystic. I mean I can tell when Stetson's angry or Adeline's upset. You can tell by their mannerisms and facial expressions."

"I don't read their anger or sadness. I read their deeper emotions. The ones they keep hidden. Like love."

A shiver ran up Delaney's spine. "That's creepy."

Mystic nodded. "Tell me about it. It's also a burden. Like right now. I hate telling you the man you love doesn't love you back. But I can't let you marry someone who is just interested in your body."

Delaney perked up. "Shane is interested in my body? You can read lust too?"

"No. But I don't need psychic powers to read the way Shane looks at you." She reached out and took Delaney's hand. "I'm sorry, Del. I hate to hurt you. But you have to break your engagement to that man."

Delaney laughed. She and Shane had been so worried about Hester seeing through their lie, they hadn't even worried about Mystic.

"It's not funny, Del," Mystic said. "You can't marry a man who doesn't love you."

Delaney sobered. "I don't love him either."

Mystic stared at her. "Then why did you agree to marry him?"

"Numerous reasons. I didn't want my brothers beating him up. I didn't want his brother getting fired. And I'm lusting after him too and don't want my family to run him off before I get a chance to have sex with him."

"So you faked your engagement?"

"Yep."

Mystic rolled her eyes and fell back on the bed. "And here I thought I was saving you. I should've known better. You're not like Buck, who is in a rush to find his one true love and get married." She lifted her head and looked at Delaney. "But I don't think you should rush into sex either, Del."

"I'm twenty-five-years-old. I wouldn't call that rushing as much as plodding along at a snail's pace. I'm ready for some hot, passionate sex. More than ready." She flopped on the bed next to Mystic. "Now all I need is some place to have it. Every time things start to get interesting, my family interrupts us."

Mystic laughed. "I can see where that would be a problem."

"A big problem. I need a sex lair. Some private place where we won't be bothered and can get as loud and wild as we want." A thought struck her. "How about the spare room in your basement?"

Mystic shook her head. "It's rented for the next

week to Dave Baker's aunt and uncle. I guess the uncle snores so loudly, Dave's wife didn't want them staying at their house."

"Shoot." Delaney blew out her breath. "I wish the foreman's house hadn't burned down. That would've made a great lovers' retreat. Not too far, but just far enough."

"Even if it hadn't burned down that house was in pretty rough shape. If you're into that rustic, you could just use the old tree house."

Delaney turned to her. "The old tree house! Why didn't I think of that?"

"I was kidding, Del."

"I'm not. No one in my family goes there anymore. With a little cleaning and a soft mattress, it would make the perfect sex lair."

Mystic cringed. "I wish I'd never said anything. I can't stand the thought of the sweet little tree house where we played as kids being used for your sexual exploits."

Delaney shot her a look. "As if you and Buck didn't do naughty things in there. I remember catching you two playing doctor."

Mystic blushed. "We were just kids."

"Well, I'm not a kid. And it's my turn to play doctor."

A strange look entered Mystic's eyes. "Be careful, Del. Sometimes just having fun can turn into something more. I don't want you to get hurt."

"I'm going into this with my eyes wide open. I won't get hurt. Especially when I have a friend who reads people's emotions. I don't know why you don't want anyone to know about your gift.

It's awesome."

"Because of the way you reacted when you first found out. Reading people's emotions isn't awesome as much as creepy. And we already have one creepy fortune-teller in the family. We don't need another."

"It is a little creepy, but I bet people would pay good money to know if their partner loves them."

"What about the times I'm wrong?" Mystic asked. "I couldn't live with myself if I ruined someone's happily ever after because I thought there wasn't love there when there was. Or vice versa."

She did have a point. Hester had made quite a few wrong predictions. But predicting a tornado and it didn't happen wasn't the same as telling someone their partner loved them when they didn't. Or didn't love them when they did.

"When you look at it like that, I guess your gift is not really a gift," Delaney said.

"Exactly. None of my family's gifts are gifts. All they've done is make people think we're a bunch of crazy witches who should be feared."

"Not you. No one thinks you're a witch, Mystic."

"Because they don't know about my weird sight. Which is why you can't say anything, Del. I don't want every person in the county being afraid of me. Or worse, coming to me for love advice."

Delaney socked Mystic in the arm. "Don't worry. Your secret is safe with me. Just like I hope my secret is safe with you."

"What secret?"

Delaney turned to see Buck standing in the doorway, holding a chewed-up straw hat. She laughed as she rolled to her feet. "It looks like you found Karl."

Buck tossed his hat onto the dresser and glanced between her and Mystic. "What secret are y'all talking about?" He grinned. "It's something for my birthday, isn't it? Well, you confided in the wrong person, Del. Mystic and I don't keep secrets from each other. Do we, Miss?"

Mystic's face seemed to lose all color as she got up from the bed. "Sometimes you have to keep a secret."

Buck's eyes widened. "But we took a blood oath to always share everything."

"We were ten, Buck."

"So? A blood oath is for life." He scooped Mystic up in his arms and flipped her onto the bed where he proceeded to tickle her until she giggled uncontrollably. "Come on, Missy, fess up. Is it the new fishing pole I wanted?"

Delaney watched their shenanigans with a touch of sadness. She had always thought Buck and Mystic belonged together and, sooner or later, they would realize it and get married. But that wasn't going to happen.

If anyone would know if there was a chance for love between Buck and Mystic, it was Mystic.

Chapter Eight

WHEN SHANE HAD first come to Cursed, posing as his brother and a prospective pastor of their church, he'd been greeted with respect and friendly smiles. But it was nothing compared to how he was treated when he drove into town today. It was like he was a celebrity. People honked and waved. He would've thought they had confused him with Chance if they hadn't also hollered out greetings.

"Hey, Shane! Welcome back."

"Good to see you, Shane!"

"Congrats, Shane!"

"You got a good one, Shane!"

When he got to the end of town, a postal truck zipped in front of him, forcing him to slam on his brakes. Kitty Carson jumped out, then hustled over to the driver's side of his truck and stuck her head in the open window.

"Hey, Shane! Glad to see you got back from Dallas." She flashed her buckteeth. "I heard you're not going back. And all I can say is praise the Lord and pass the biscuits. Everyone in town would've cried their eyes out if you had taken our little

Delaney away from Cursed. This is her home." She thumped his shoulder. "Now it's yours. We're just pleased as punch to have another Kingman to love." She pinned him with a hard stare. "So? Did you get the ring?"

"Uhh . . . no, not yet. I'm going to let Delaney pick it out."

"Well, that's all fine and good. But just between you and me, that's no way to start a marriage. We women don't want to pick out our own rings. We want our men to know us well enough to pick out the perfect ring for us. Bernard gave me the ugliest engagement ring you ever did see. He got it cheap from old Miss Helmsley when he fixed her toilet. And that's where our marriage went. Straight down the toilet. What you think of a woman shows in the ring you give her. Delaney is no ordinary woman. She's going to need something original. Something unique."

"You're right. I need to find something original and unique—no matter how long it takes."

Kitty squinted. "Well, now, you don't want to take too long. A girl will only wait so long for an engagement ring before she thinks her man is cheap. Or got cold feet." She shook her head. "No, you can't wait. You need to find that ring and you need to find that ring soon."

Since he couldn't think of anything to say that wouldn't give away their charade, he just sat there.

"Now don't look so defeated." Kitty patted his arm. "I got your back. I'm gonna help you find that ring."

"Oh, you don't need to—"

"Nonsense. I can't have you giving our little Delaney something she won't love as much as she loves you. You just leave it to me. I'll find you a ring that will light that little girl's eyes up. Now, I better get back to work. Neither sleet nor hail nor engagement rings can keep the Cursed mail from being delivered." She hustled back to her truck and took off.

Shane sat there for a minute trying to figure out how he was going to stop Kitty from wasting her time when someone hollered.

"I don't blame you! That woman makes everyone feel stunned and confused."

He glanced over at the large farmhouse. According to what Chance had told him, the Malones' house was the oldest house in town. It certainly didn't look it. The house had been well cared for. The siding wasn't warped or weather beaten and was painted a pristine white. The shutters were painted a deep navy and the door a bright red. While the house was bright, Hester Malone sat on the porch wearing her usual solid black.

She waved a hand at him. Not in greeting, but in "come here."

The last thing he wanted to do was talk to Hester. If anyone was going to figure out the charade, it was she. Pretending like he thought she was just waving, he waved back and hit the gas. Unfortunately, his old truck chose that moment to overheat. The engine sputtered before it died. It usually took a good five minutes before it would cool down and start back up.

"Car trouble?" Hester hollered.

"It just needs to cool off," he hollered back.

"Might as well come on up to the porch while you wait."

With no other choice, Shane left his truck sitting in the middle of the street and walked up the path that led to the porch. When he reached it, he took off his hat and tried to avoid eye contact by looking up at the sky. "Hey, Ms. Malone. Enjoying this fine day?"

"It will rain tonight."

He nodded and looked at the hot-pink flowers growing in front of the porch. "We can sure use it."

There was a long pause before she spoke. "You don't have to hide from me. Whatever secrets I see, I don't repeat."

He kept his gaze lowered. "Well, that's nice to hear. But I don't really have any secrets."

"Of course you do. Everyone has secrets. Even I do."

He couldn't help glancing up. Her violet eyes were as piercing as always, but they also held a kindness that reminded him of his grandmother.

"Come sit down, Shane Ransom," she said. "I don't tell people things they aren't ready to hear. And you're not quite ready to hear what the future holds for you."

"You see my future?"

"You sound skeptical."

Shane moved up the steps of the porch and took a chair next to her. "I'm sure you're more intuitive than most people. But no one can predict the future because no one can predict human nature.

Every decision we make changes the course of our lives."

"Exactly true. Which is why I share my visions and dreams. I want people to change their course if they're headed for the rocks."

"Am I headed for rocks?"

"No. Just rough waters. But I think you're the type of man who can navigate them. I'm not worried about you." She hesitated. "I am worried about your brother."

Shane tensed. "Chance? Why?"

"Did he lose someone recently?"

Okay, so maybe the woman was more than intuitive. "He lost his wife in a car accident over a year ago. A drunk driver hit them head on. Then our grandmother died a few months later. But Chance has a lot of faith so I don't think there's any reason to worry about him."

"It's his faith he's struggling with."

Shane stared at her with stunned shock. "Chance is struggling with his faith?" His brother's faith had always been something Shane counted on. "Are you sure?"

Hester nodded. "Which is why I'm glad you're sticking around. He needs your support."

"I'm not sure I'd be much help in the faith department."

"I disagree. When I look at you, I see a man of strong faith." She paused. "Your only fault is spending too much time worshipping the wrong god. Money will get you things, but not the things you need the most."

This woman did have some kind of psychic

powers. One part of him wanted to run for the hills, and the other part wanted to know more. "And what do I need the most, Ms. Malone?"

"That's for you to figure out. And you will. For now, you need to be there for your brother."

He wanted to ask her what she'd seen about Chance. But before he could, Mystic stepped out the door.

"I'm going to run some errands, Hessy. I'll be back—" She cut off when she saw Shane. "Oh, I didn't realize we had company. Shane?"

He nodded and got to his feet. "You can usually tell by the hair. I need a haircut in a bad way."

"Then you've come to the right spot. I cut hair for a living. I'd be happy to set you up with an appointment. I can't fit you in this week. But I can next."

"That would be great."

She waved a hand as she headed down the steps. "Come on around to my salon and I'll see what openings I have."

He glanced at Hester. "I'll be right back."

"No need to come back. I told you all you need to know." Completely dismissing him, she headed inside, the screen door slamming behind her.

"I hope she wasn't making any wild predictions," Mystic said when he joined her at the bottom of the porch steps. "Hessy has always been overly dramatic."

"She was just asking me about my brother."

"Is your brother okay?"

Not wanting to get into the details, he kept it simple. "He's going through a rough patch, but

I'm sure he'll be fine."

Except Shane wasn't sure. After talking with Hester, he was more than a little worried about Chance. Lost his faith? When Chance had quit his pastoring job in Austin, Shane had just thought he needed a break. He hadn't thought his brother had lost his faith. If Hester was right, things were not good. They weren't good at all. Chance had always been the stable one—the one who kept Shane grounded. Knowing his brother carried on their grandmother's faith had always been a touchstone for Shane. Something he relied on. He might stumble in life, but Chance never would.

Now Chance was stumbling and it scared Shane.

He was still thinking about his brother when he stepped into the Cursed Cut and Curl. The salon was like stepping into a girlie nightmare. The walls were lavender striped, the chairs purple, the couch white with fuzzy pillows, and the floor black-and-white checkered.

Shane instantly felt out of place. "I'm going to assume you don't get a lot of rough cowboys in here."

Mystic laughed. "Most of the rough cowboys go to the barber in town. Except for Buck." For some reason, she blushed before she directed her attention to the screen of the laptop sitting on the appointment counter. "I have a nine o'clock on the Tuesday after next open."

"That will work," Shane said.

She typed in his name, then clicked the screen

back to today's schedule. It looked like it was full so he decided not to keep her.

"Thanks for getting me in. I'll let you get to those errands." He turned to leave, but she stopped him.

"Delaney isn't as tough as she lets on."

He turned back to her and lifted his eyebrows in question. "Excuse me?"

Mystic hesitated before she spoke. "I don't want her getting hurt, Shane."

"I have no intentions of hurting Delaney."

Mystic moved out from behind the appointment counter. "Sometimes you can unintentionally hurt someone. And I thought if you knew more about Delaney, it would help you to keep from doing that. A lot of people think she's a cowgirl princess, but Del hasn't had an easy life. She lost her mother when she was four. Her father when she was twelve. She was raised by Stetson and Adeline, who hadn't even finished college, and who also had the responsibility of keeping a huge ranch going. Buck and Delaney had to grow up quickly. They were expected to help with the ranch and go to school and get good grades. Stetson made sure Wolfe, Buck, and Delaney got to go to college, but they didn't get to be fun-loving college kids. Every weekend and every summer, they came back to the ranch to help out. They weren't forced to, but they felt a responsibility to the ranch and their family. They still do. It wasn't so bad for Buck and Wolfe. They get to blow off steam with the other ranch hands and in town on the weekends."

She snorted. "Believe me, Buck and Wolfe have blown off plenty of steam. But Delaney isn't so lucky."

"What do you mean? It seems to me that she gets to do whatever she wants. Including frequenting Nasty Jack's."

"She might get a little drunk and shoot a little pool, but no one at the ranch or in town would ever touch Delaney Kingman. Not only because they don't want to piss off her family, but also because they don't want to piss off the townsfolk."

It took him a moment to digest what Mystic was saying. "Wait a second. Are you saying I'm Delaney's first boyfriend?"

"She's dated. But yes, you're her first serious relationship." Mystic sighed. "She would kill me if she found out I'd told you. I just thought you needed to know before you two . . ." She shook her head. "Look, I probably shouldn't have said anything. You're both adults and what you choose to do together is your business. I'm just concerned for my friend." She picked up her keys and headed for the door. "Now, I better get to those errands."

Shane followed her out in a daze. He was Delaney's first real boyfriend? What exactly did that mean?

When he got to his truck, it started up right away. But he didn't put it into drive. He just sat there trying to make sense of what Mystic had told him. She had to be mistaken. How could a woman who was as beautiful and outgoing as

Delaney not have had plenty of relationships?

Needing answers, he pulled his cellphone from his pocket. Delaney had given him her number before he'd left for Dallas, but this was the first time he'd used it. She didn't answer so he left a message.

"It's Shane. We need to talk."

He hung up and headed toward the ranch. On the way, Delaney called back.

"Sorry I didn't pick up. I didn't recognize the number." She laughed. "I guess I need to put you on my contact list. So what's up? 'We need to talk' sounded pretty ominous."

He started to question her, but then decided it would be best if they had this discussion in person. "We'll talk when I get there."

"Get here? You're on your way to the ranch?"

"About twenty minutes away."

"Twenty minutes? That doesn't give me much time."

"Much time for what?"

"Never mind. I'll see you soon. Oh! And don't go to the house. I'm at the tree house. Just head to the stables and make a left, then go about a half mile down the road and you'll see a cluster of trees on your right. My truck will be parked there. Walk straight to the biggest oak and look up."

"What are you doing in a tree house?"

"Playing house, of course." She laughed before she hung up.

Her directions turned out to be exact. A little over twenty minutes later, he pulled up to a cluster of trees right next to a newer red GMC truck. In the very center of the trees, he found a huge oak with the most amazing tree house he had ever seen in his life sitting amid the branches. It had actual glass windows with shutters that had been branded with the Kingman Ranch brand. A tiny little balcony with miniature French doors and two kid-sized rocking chairs. And instead of a simple rope ladder that you had to climb to get to the tree house, there was a winding staircase around the thick trunk of the tree.

Chase followed the narrow wood steps with the rope bannister to a small door that resembled a hobbit's. Except this one had a horseshoe door knocker. He tapped it and Delaney's voice drifted out.

"Come in."

He opened the door.

The sight that greeted him took his breath away.

Chapter Nine

As Shane continued to stand there without saying a word, Delaney started to wonder if maybe she should have given him a little warning about her plans. She had wanted to surprise him, but she hadn't wanted to stun him into silence.

Obviously, she had done something wrong. She had looked up "setting a seductive scene" online and followed all the tips. She'd stored all the kid toys in the chest and purchased one of those mattresses in a box online and covered it in soft cotton sheets, multiple throw pillows, and a puffy down comforter. After she'd gotten off the phone with Shane, she'd taken the fastest shower ever and was all shaved and fresh as a daisy.

And naked as the day she was born.

Since she had never been naked as the day she was born with any man, she felt extremely uncomfortable and embarrassed. But she wasn't about to let Shane know that. She had come up with this plan and she was going to see it through. No matter how much she wanted to dive under the comforter and never come out.

"Hey, stranger. Welcome home."

Shane opened his mouth as if to speak, but nothing came out as his gaze wandered over her body. And maybe that was a good thing. Maybe her naked beauty had struck him speechless. Still, it would make her feel a lot better if he said something. Anything.

Unable to take the silence a second more, she sat up. "So are you going to say something?" She smiled. "Or maybe do something? Like come over here and kiss me."

His mouth closed, and he looked away. "We need to talk, Delaney."

That's exactly what he'd said on the phone. She figured he just wanted to go over the rules of their fake engagement. Get their stories straight. But that could wait.

"How about we talk later."

He shook his head and continued to stare out the window. "No. We need to talk now. How many boyfriends have you had?"

She blinked, completely confused. "Boyfriends?"

"Yes. How many relationships have you been in?"

She tried to figure out where the question had come from and why he was acting so weird, and then it hit her. "Oh! You're worried I might have something catching. Well, you don't have to worry about that."

"And why is that?" He looked back at her, then turned away again. "Do you think you could cover up?"

This was not going the way she had planned. "You want me to cover up?"

"Yes. I can't think when you're naked."

Suddenly, she felt a lot less self-conscious. Her plan was obviously working. He was just being cautious. She was pleased he was the type of man who was concerned about safety and health. She should have thought more about that herself.

She grabbed the edge of the comforter and pulled it over her. "There. I'm decent. Or not really decent as much as covered."

He looked back at her and his relief was obvious. "Thank you."

"You're welcome." She stuffed a few pillows behind her head and reclined back, making sure to leave just enough cleavage on view to keep him interested. "Now what has you so worried? I don't have any diseases. And as far as contraception goes, I brought condoms and I've been on birth control ever since I decided to lose my virginity."

"And when exactly did you lose your virginity?"

She frowned. "Do you always ask so many questions before you have sex with a woman?"

"When, Delaney? And with whom?"

She tried to bluff her way through. "A long time ago with a ranch hand."

"Hmm? And he didn't worry about losing his job and getting his ass kicked by your brothers?"

"He was just passing through."

"What was his name?"

She scrambled through her mind for a name.

"Red Pollard." As soon as the words came out of her mouth, she wanted them back. Of course, she probably had nothing to worry about. A computer nerd wouldn't know anything about racehorses or remember a character's name from a horse movie.

Unfortunately, she was wrong.

Shane's eyes narrowed. "Red Pollard? The jockey who rode Seabiscuit?"

Damn. "This was a different Red Pollard."

Shane studied her for a long moment before he sighed and ran a hand through his hair. "Why didn't you tell me?"

Realizing the jig was up, she punched the comforter with both her fists. "Who told you?"

"It doesn't matter who told me. What matters is that you didn't."

"What difference does it make?"

His eyes flashed with anger. "A helluva lot of difference. It's not just two people having sex. It's one person experiencing sex for the first time. That's a lot of responsibility for the other person."

"And I'm assuming by your anger that you don't want that responsibility."

"Hell, no, I don't want the responsibility! I thought when you hopped into my truck at Nasty Jack's you knew what you were doing."

"I did know what I was doing."

He snorted. "Yeah, you were looking for a fool who didn't know who you were to gift your virginity to. Well, I don't want it. I'm not looking to be someone's first-time experiment in sex."

She didn't know if it was hurt or disappointment that made her anger flare. Either way, she was pissed. She threw back the comforter and jumped to her feet. Shane's eyes widened, but she didn't care about his tender sensibilities anymore.

"So that's it? You aren't going to bed with me because I'm a virgin? That is such bullshit! Did you tell the first person you had sex with that you were a virgin?" She snorted as she picked up her panties and pulled them on. "Of course you didn't. You probably acted like you had been with lots of other girls and were a real stud. And yet, here you are on your high horse, acting like I am so wicked for not sharing the information with you."

"I was a stupid kid. You're an adult."

"And that's the point!" She jerked on her jeans. "I'm an adult who doesn't want to be the virgin princess anymore. I want to experience life. All of life. Instead, I'm stuck in a Podunk town with a bunch of wussy men who are too scared to have sex with me. And when I finally find a man who isn't too scared of my family, he's got some kind of weird morals about having sex with a virgin."

"They aren't weird. It's one thing to have sex with an experienced woman and quite another to have sex with an inexperienced one. I don't want you forming any attachments and expecting this engagement to be more than it is."

She froze in the process of zipping her jeans. "So that's it. You're worried I'm going to fall in love with you and refuse to break off the engagement." She laughed. "You certainly think a lot of yourself, Shane Ransom. But you don't have to worry about me falling for you. I'm only interested in one thing." She gave him a thorough once-over. "Your body." When his jaw tightened, she shrugged. "Come on, Shane. Don't try to act like you were interested in more than my body. We don't even know each other."

"You're right. So why me? Why did you pick me? You can't tell me other men who didn't know who you were haven't come to Cursed."

He had a good point. There had been other strangers she'd run into at Nasty Jack's. Men who didn't know who she was or who her family was. And yet, she hadn't hopped in their trucks. She hadn't thought about their kisses day and night. Or gone to Hester Malone to get help finding them. There was something about Shane. Something that wasn't just physical attraction. And maybe it was the same thing that was keeping her from getting what she wanted.

His damn morality.

"Obviously, I made a bad choice. Next time I'll choose someone who isn't so persnickety." She grabbed her bra and shirt and started putting them on.

"I'm sure you can find a lot of men who aren't as . . . persnickety if you left Cursed. Why don't you?"

"Leave?" She finished pulling on her shirt and stared at him. "I can't leave my family."

"Why not? Everyone leaves their family eventually."

"Well, Kingmans don't." She sat down on the mattress to put on her socks and boots. "It takes a lot of people to run a ranch the size of this one. I can't just up and run off. You talked about responsibilities. Well, you don't know the meaning of the word. Everyone in my family has made sacrifices to keep this ranch going and the family together. I won't be any different." She finished tugging on her boots and stood. "Now if you'll excuse me, I have work to do. You no longer have to worry about me not breaking our engagement. As far as I'm concerned, it's over. I'd give you back your ring, but I never got one."

She headed for the door, but he took her arm and stopped her. "Wait a second. You're breaking our engagement because I won't go to bed with you?"

"Yep. That was the one perk of being engaged. Now that it's off the table, I don't see the appeal of being your fake fiancée a second longer."

His eyes darkened. "And what about my brother? If we break up this quickly, people in town are going to know it was just a ruse."

"I'll take full blame."

"It's too late for that. I've already lied to Kitty Carson. I can't have her holding my lies against Chance. He needs his job more than ever." He shook his head. "No. We're staying engaged. At least, for another few weeks."

"Like hell we are." She went to move around him, but he blocked her exit.

"This entire thing was your idea. You talk about how much your family means to you. Well, my brother means a lot to me. I won't have him hurt because a spoiled little rich girl wanted to play at being a woman."

Now it wasn't anger that Delaney felt. It was more out-and-out rage.

"I am a woman!" She doubled up her fist and let it fly. But Shane caught her wrist before it could connect with his jaw. She swung her other fist, but he caught that too and pushed her back against the wall.

If any other man had done that to Delaney, she would've kneed him in the groin and come out swinging. She had wrestled all her life with her brothers and knew exactly how to win a fight with a man. But there was something about the press of Shane's body that melted all her resistance.

She stopped struggling and lifted her gaze to his. There was anger in the soft brown of his eyes, but there was also something else. Something hot and needy that spoke to the hot and needy feeling growing inside of her.

They both moved at the same time, their mouths meeting in a hungry tangle of lips and tongues. His hands lightened on her wrists he held over her head, his thumbs stroking her pulse that seeming to be throbbing out of control. She flexed her hips, rubbing against the press of his hard body as she nipped at his bottom lip and pulled it between her teeth. He groaned and his hips joined hers in a bump and grind that had her struggling to catch her breath.

Then suddenly, his hips stopped moving and he pulled away from the kiss and released her. Their breath heaved in and out of their lungs as they stared at one another. He looked as stunned by the force of what had just happened as she was. But he recovered quickly.

He leaned down and scooped up his hat from the floor before he looked back at her. "We're not breaking the engagement." He turned and walked out.

When he was gone, Delaney slid down the wall until her butt hit the floor. She didn't have a clue what had just happened.

But whatever it was, she wanted more.

One way or another, she was going to get it.

Chapter Ten

Shane stood outside the door of the tree house, feeling dazed and confused. Not just about Delaney being a virgin, but also about the passion that had just ignited between them. He knew he had chemistry with Delaney. That was obvious from their very first kiss. But this was something else. Something stronger and more primitive. Maybe it had to do with seeing her naked for the first time.

Delaney had one fine body.

Her arms and legs were toned with the lean muscle you can only get from working a ranch. Her breasts were small and high with soft pink nipples that almost blended with the pale skin that had never seen the sun. When she'd turned to search for her clothes, Shane had been treated to a curvy backside that had made his mouth go dry.

Saying no to her delectable body had been one of the hardest things he'd ever done in his life. Especially when their kiss had red-hot lust exploding inside him.

But he couldn't give in to his lust. The stakes

were too high.

Having sex with Delaney would no longer be just a fun interlude. He would be her first sexual partner. While some men might take pride in being a woman's first, Shane did not. Sex could convolute your emotions—especially if you weren't experienced. After having sex his first time, he'd fallen head over heels for Jackie Adams. He'd been devastated when she'd dropped him for the star football player.

Then there was his college friend, Everly Grayson. He'd thought they could just have one night of casual sex, but it had complicated their entire relationship when Everly had started having feelings for him. It had almost ruined their friendship. What would happen if Delaney fell in love with Shane? If he broke her heart, the entire town would want to string him up. If not him, then Chance. He didn't doubt for a second that if he hurt Delaney, Chance would lose his pastoring position.

Not to mention Shane would feel like crap for taking advantage of an inexperienced woman. No, it was best if he and Delaney didn't complicate their fake engagement with the emotions that came with first-time sex.

He wished they could break off the engagement now. But after what Hester had told him, he couldn't chance the town thinking they had lied about everything and blaming Chance. Chance needed a congregation of believers surrounding him right now.

If Shane was honest, there was another reason

he didn't want to break off the engagement. Dan Fuller hadn't been interested in investing in his company until he'd asked Shane some questions about his personal life and Shane had dropped the Kingman name. The Kingman Ranch was one of the biggest in the country and its name held power—especially in the Texas business world. Once Dan had found out about Shane's engagement to Delaney, he'd perked up and listened more intently. He hadn't agreed to invest in Shane's app, but he had said that he'd think about it. Which was more than Shane had gotten before. He shouldn't have used the Kingman name, but he figured it wouldn't hurt anything. All he needed was a little financial help to get his app launched.

Until then, Shane and Delaney needed to keep up the farce. Which would be difficult if Delaney refused to play along.

As much as he didn't want to, he needed to go back inside the tree house and make sure they were on the same page. He turned to open the door when Delaney stepped out. She looked like she had been thoroughly kissed. Her hair was mussed and her cheeks flushed and her lips puffy. Damn, if he didn't want to pull her into his arms and kiss her again. Thankfully, before he could do something stupid, she pushed past him.

"Come on, I'll take you up to the house and show you your room."

Surprised she'd conceded so easily, it took Shane a moment before he followed her down the steps. She might be willing to go along with the fake engagement, but it was obvious she wasn't happy about it. By the time he reached the bottom of the stairs, she was leaving him in a trail of dust. When he got to Buckinghorse Palace, she was waiting by the back door for him. Without saying a word, she led him inside where they left their cowboy hats on hooks in the mudroom before heading up the huge staircase to the second floor.

The guestroom with its en suite bathroom was bigger than Shane's Dallas apartment. It had a king-sized bed, a small sitting area with a desk, and French doors that led out to a balcony with an amazing view of the garden. He dropped his duffel on the upholstered bench at the end of the bed and turned to her.

"This is very nice. Thank you."

"You're welcome." She hesitated. "My room is just three doors down on your right. Just in case you were wondering."

Since it was information he could've done without, he merely nodded as he unzipped his bag and took out his laptop and charger. He'd already lost most of the day. He needed to get to work. He was hoping she'd get the hint and leave when he set up his laptop on the desk. She didn't.

"So you're really not going to have sex with me."

He glanced back at her. "I think it's for the best."

"And I think having sex is for the best. But I guess we're all allowed our own opinions." She hesitated. "Or to change them."

"I won't change mine." He knelt to plug in his

charger.

"Are you sure? Because I kinda got the feeling you were waffling in the tree house."

He sighed and turned to her. "Look, Delaney. I'm not going to pretend like I don't desire you. We both know I do. But you don't want your first time to be with a man you don't even know."

"So it's okay for me to have sex with a man I don't know as long as it's not my first time?"

She had a good point. He had been willing to have sex with her when he'd thought she was experienced. "You're right. It's never a good idea to have sex with someone you don't know. And you don't know me. So let's leave it at that and move on." He sat down at the desk and booted up his laptop.

"So who are you, Shane Ransom?"

He couldn't help but smile. She was persistent. But he could be persistent too. "Someone who has work to do." He took the AirPods out of his pocket, put them in his ears, and tapped on his playlist. Then he focused his attention on his laptop. Or tried to. It was hard to focus when his mind kept wandering to the tree house kiss. It took awhile before he was able to concentrate and get some work done. He didn't know how long he had been at the computer when Siri informed him of an incoming text from Chance.

Are you in town?

He had told his brother about coming to live on the Kingman Ranch. While Chance was happy about Shane living closer, he was still leery about the entire engagement and kept trying to pin Shane down for a time they could talk. They did need to talk. Just not about Shane's engagement. They needed to talk about Chance losing his faith. Although Shane didn't have a clue how he could help his brother in that department. Maybe Hester was right. Maybe he didn't need to say anything. He just needed to be there for Chance.

He told Siri what to reply. "I got to the ranch. I'll call you later and we can figure out a time to meet up."

When the text was sent, he took out his AirPods and lifted his arms over his head to stretch. As he twisted, he glanced behind him. His eyes widened. He'd thought Delaney had left. Instead, she was lying on his bed . . . fast asleep. He sighed and got up. His plan was to wake her and get her to leave. But she was sleeping so soundly, he couldn't do it.

She slept at an awkward angle with her boots hanging off the side of the bed and her head on the pillows. He carefully pulled off her boots before he tucked her feet under the folded down comforter, then pulled it over her. He stepped back and smiled at the picture she presented. There was no doubt she was beautiful. Her features needed no makeup to enhance them. Her rich black hair needed no highlights or professional styling.

But it was her personality that had first drawn him in the bar. The mixture of feisty cowgirl and flirting woman. He'd been intrigued from the moment she'd pointed her pool cue at him and said, "Well, don't just sit there lookin' pretty, cowboy. Step up and show me what ya got." He had played pool all through college and had been so certain he could best her. She had made him feel like an amateur. Stetson had said she was just as good at poker. He could see her wanting to be good at everything she did.

An image of her naked popped into his head. He couldn't help thinking about how good she'd be in bed.

"She's not sleeping in here until you're married."

The low, growling words had Shane turning to see Wolfe standing in the doorway. Did the two older Kingman brothers always wear scowls?

Shane pinned on a smile. "I don't expect her to." There was no way he could resist her if she slept in the same bed with him. "She just fell asleep while I was working."

Wolfe glanced at his sister and the scowl melted into confusion. "That's weird. Delaney hates naps. When she was little, I'd spend hours reading to her or singing songs she liked and she never once dozed off."

Shane didn't find Delaney's napping habits as strange as the fact that Wolfe had read and sang to her. He knew their mother had died when Delaney was little, but why hadn't their father put her down for a nap and read to her?

"I wasn't much for naps either," Shane said. "Chance would fall right to sleep and I would pretend to be asleep until my grandmother left the room and then I'd get up and play."

Wolfe looked back at Shane. "I don't like this entire fast engagement thing."

According to Chance, fast engagements ran in the family—and fast marriages. But Shane refused to point that out to a man who looked like he would enjoy using Shane's face as a punching bag. "I can understand that. I'm sure our engagement came as a surprise. But while we got engaged quickly, we're in no rush to get married."

Wolfe's eyes narrowed. "And why is that?"

He gave him the same answer he'd given Stetson. "We want to make sure we're compatible."

"Shouldn't you have figured that out before you got engaged?"

Thankfully, before he had to come up with an answer, Delaney sat up. "Stop browbeating my fiancé, Wolfe." She yawned widely and blinked. "What happened? Did I fall asleep?"

"You were out like a light." Wolfe's eyes held concern as he walked over and placed a hand on her forehead. "Are you okay, Del? You do feel a little warm?"

Delaney batted his hand away. "I'm fine. What time is it?"

"Suppertime." Wolfe glanced at Shane. "I'll have Potts set another plate."

"Thank you, but I have work to do," Shane said. "I'll just grab something later."

"That's not how it works in this house," Wolfe said. "You can do whatever you want for lunch, but breakfast and dinner are eaten together or not at all."

Delaney shot him a wide smile. "Welcome to

the Kingman Ranch."

Shane had figured meals would be eaten in the huge dining room, but the Kingmans seemed to prefer to eat at the harvest table in the kitchen. Tonight, two separate conversations seemed to be going on—the women were talking about a baby shower for Adeline and the men were talking about horses. When Wolfe, Delaney, and Shane stepped in, all talking ceased and every eye turned to Shane. Before he could apologize for not giving them warning about his arrival, Delaney spoke.

"Surprise! My fiancé decided to come back early from Dallas. I guess he just couldn't stay away from his one true love." She smacked his butt. "Isn't that right, honey buns?"

He knew she was trying to get back at him for not having sex with her. He also knew if he showed any kind of embarrassment, her teasing would only get worse. So he tugged her into his arms for a quick kiss. "That's right, sugar pea. I just couldn't live without my sassy cowgirl."

A flicker of surprise entered her clear blue eyes, but the surprise quickly faded to be replaced with determination. As soon as he saw it, he realized his mistake. He'd just upped the stakes. Delaney wasn't the type to fold.

She looped her arms around his neck and gave him a kiss that made his face burn . . . and his body. When she drew back, she sighed dramatically. "You'll never have to live without me. I'm going to stick to you like gum on a shoe."

Buck groaned. "I think I'm going to be sick.

Can I be excused? I'd rather eat in my room than endure one more second of this."

"No one is eating in their room." Stetson got to his feet. "Come join us, Shane. Buck, move over so Delaney can sit next to her fiancé."

Buck got up and Shane pulled out a chair for Delaney before he took the chair Buck had just vacated. There was a moment of uncomfortable awkwardness before Potts spoke. "Well, don't just sit there looking at each other. I don't slave away in this kitchen for my food to get cold."

Potts's cooking was delicious . . . and plentiful. There were two kinds of casseroles—one with chicken and one with ground beef—and more side dishes than Shane could count. For a man who usually got his food delivered to his door cold, it was a real treat. He even enjoyed listening to the dinner conversation. The Kingmans were an opinionated group who argued and fought over just about everything. But they did it with obvious love. Delaney had her own opinions too. Especially about the running of the ranch. Unfortunately, no one seemed to take them seriously.

At first, Shane thought it had to do with her being a woman. But then he noticed that no one listened to Buck either. The two youngest Kingmans were treated like they were new apprentices in a business. Which made no sense if what Mystic said was true and Buck and Delaney had been working the ranch ever since they'd been kids.

Shane was still pondering the weird family dynamic when the feel of a hand sliding up his thigh had him choking on the bite of fried potatoes he'd just taken.

Uncle Jack, who sat on his other side, thumped him on the back. "You okay, boy?"

He cleared his throat and grabbed Delaney's wandering hand before it reached his fly. "I'm good." He gave Uncle Jack a tight smile before he glanced at Delaney.

She smiled innocently. "You shouldn't eat so quickly, honey buns. I wouldn't want to lose you after I just got you."

For the rest of the meal and all through dessert, Delaney's hand kept wandering. By the time dinner was over, Shane was more than ready to leave the table and escape to his room . . . where he could take a cold shower.

But Stetson had other ideas. "Let's all go into the family room. Lily and I have an announcement to make."

Once everyone was gathered around the massive fireplace, Stetson took Lily's hand and drew her close. A smile lit his face. Since Shane had rarely seen the man smile, he was a little taken back by the transformation. "We hate to steal your and Gage's thunder, Addie," Stetson said. "But it looks like there's going to be two new additions to our family." He looked down at his wife and beamed. "Lily's pregnant."

Hoots and celebratory congratulations erupted before Wolfe played bartender and got everyone drinks to toast the soon-to-be parents. After the toast, Shane figured it was a good time to slip out and let the family continue their celebration without him.

He made it all the way up the stairs when Delaney's voice stopped him.

"And just where are you runnin' off to?"

He turned and watched as she came up the stairs toward him. "I'm going to my room. I have some work to do."

She stopped on the stair below his and gave him a sassy smirk. "Have you ever heard the old adage about all work and no play?"

"We aren't going to play, Delaney." No matter how much his body wanted to.

She ran her finger along the open neck of his shirt. It was amazing how one little caress could set him on fire. "Not even a little?"

He held firm. "Not even a little."

A smile tipped her mouth. "Whatever you say, honey buns." She leaned in and kissed him with a slide of hot lips and wet tongue before she turned and headed down the stairs.

It was going to be a long two weeks.

Chapter Eleven

Delaney always got plenty of attention when she went into Cursed. The old women pinched her cheeks and gifted her with cookies. The old men issued warnings about young men and bought her popsicles and suckers. The young women all treated her like their annoying kid sister and barely said "hi." And the young men usually ran like hell.

But today, things were different.

Mrs. Humphries invited her to join the women's wine tasting club, Wining Women. Old Mr. Phelps stopped her at the grocery store to ask her if she knew any octogenarian ladies who were still sexually active. Karla Joe Filkins ran into her on the street and acted like they were best friends and said she'd be happy to be her bridesmaid. And, at the gas station, Josh Michaels actually winked and flirted with her.

It was like she had grown up overnight. It was weird and annoying as hell.

Something she had no problem expressing when she stepped into Mystic's salon.

"I swear the townsfolk are as crazy as bedbugs!"

She froze when she saw Kitty Carson sitting in one of the salon chairs. But while Kitty talked about everyone else, she never thought people were talking about her.

"Amen to that!" she said. "And they just get crazier every day. Did you hear about Vern White's fetish for cat toys? Mildred Pike said he bought at least fifty dollars' worth at the Cursed Market and he doesn't even own a cat. And then there's Mike Rogers, who said he went up in a UFO and learned how to make alien sauerkraut. I tasted it. Just tasted like plain ol' sauerkraut to me." She looked in the mirror and touched her stiff helmet of red hair. "I think I need more hairspray, Mystic."

"You sure?" Mystic asked. "I think you're good."

Kitty took the can from her. "A dedicated postal worker has to deal with rain, snow, sleet, and stiff Texas wind. I can't have any of those messing up my do." She sprayed a cloud around her as Mystic stood back and covered her nose and mouth. After a full minute, she stopped spraying and smiled at herself in the mirror. "Perfect. How much do I owe you?"

While they settled up, Delaney flopped down on the couch in the lobby and thumbed through one of the magazines. She had never been one to care about how her hair looked, but she had never been dead set on seducing a man before either. A man who was playing hard to get.

For the last three days, Delaney had done her best to get Shane in bed, but to no avail. She'd even waited until everyone was asleep and slipped down to his room. The door had been locked tight. She might've thought he was asleep if she hadn't heard fingers tapping on a keyboard. When she knocked, the tapping stopped, but he didn't answer. Even after numerous knocks—and some hard pounding—he refused to unlock the door.

Delaney was starting to wonder if she was ever going to get him into bed.

"I'm glad I ran into you, Delaney." Kitty cut into her thoughts. "I need your help."

Delaney looked up from the hairstyling magazine. "What can I do for you, Miss Kitty?"

Kitty pulled a handful of rings out of her pocket. "Would you try these rings on? I'm getting one for my mama for Mother's Day and I want to make sure it's the right size."

"How do you know we have the same size fingers?"

"Because I have a thing about fingers. Yours are identical to my mama's."

If it had been anyone but Kitty Carson, Delaney might have continued to question her. But she didn't want to hear the long story about how Kitty had come by her finger-sizing abilities. She took the rings and started slipping them on her fingers.

"Just on your left ring finger," Kitty said.

Delaney didn't understand why that finger, but she complied. Most were too big and a few were too small. Kitty nabbed the ones that didn't fit. The one that did fit was ugly as hell, but Delaney didn't get a chance to say that before Kitty slipped the ring off her finger.

"That looks like the one. Well, thanks, Delaney. And thanks for the cut, Mystic. See you gals later." She grabbed her mailbag that was sitting by the door and hooked it over her shoulder. Before she headed out, she paused and pointed a finger at Delaney. "The Cursed Ladies' Auxiliary Club is meeting at Nasty Jack's next Friday, you need to be there. Now that you're all grown up, it's time for you to be part of the town's ladies' club."

When she was gone, Delaney looked at Mystic. "See what I mean. Crazier than bedbugs. What was up with the rings? And Kitty has never once invited me to join the ladies' club. Now suddenly that I'm an engaged lady, I get a coveted invitation."

"I invited you to join the ladies' club, and you told me that you'd rather be bit by a rattlesnake than waste your time drinking wine and gossiping with the ladies of this town."

"Damn straight. But my point is that everyone in town thinks I suddenly aged ten years just because I got engaged."

"Fake engaged."

"Fine. Fake engaged."

Mystic shrugged. "What can I say? You have always been the baby Kingman princess. It's hard for folks to see past that. Lord only knows what will happen when you and Shane break up."

"I'll probably become twelve again. But we don't have to worry about that for a while. I refuse to break up with the man until he gives me what I want."

"So I take it the sex lair didn't work."

"It was a fiasco. Someone—I'm betting Buck—told him I was a virgin." When Mystic's face turned bright red, Delaney eyes widened. "Mystic Twilight Malone, you didn't?"

Mystic held up her hands. "I didn't tell him you were a virgin. I just mentioned you hadn't had a lot of experience with relationships. I'm sorry, Del. But I don't want you getting hurt. I know for a fact he's not interested in you for anything but a good time."

"And I'm not interested in him for anything but a good time. So that makes us perfect sexual partners." She frowned. "If I can get him to stop being so morally upstanding and take me to bed. Which is why I'm here. I want one of those makeovers like you gave Gretchen. It worked on my brother and he was dead set against going to bed with Gretchen."

"Because he had feelings for her. He just wasn't aware of them. It had nothing to do with my haircut."

"I don't agree. And don't act like you don't want to. You've been bugging me to let you cut my hair since the last time you ruined it."

Mystic stared at her. "We were seven, Del, and those school scissors were dull."

Delaney got up and walked over to the salon chair and flopped down. "Just don't make me look like Miss Kitty."

Mystic hesitated for a second before she walked over and opened a drawer. "Fine. You want a makeover, Delaney Kingman, I'm going to give you a makeover." She shook out a purple cape and snapped it around Delaney's neck . . . a little too tight. "Now be quiet and let the master work."

For the next hour and a half, Delaney was put through all kinds of torture. Her hair was scrubbed until her scalp tingled and then a thick, gooey mask was applied and she had to sit still for a good fifteen minutes while it "worked its magic." She was not good at sitting still. Then the goop was rinsed off and Mystic combed out her hair and started cutting.

Delaney had trimmed her own hair since Mystic's second grade cut and only a couple times a year. And only a tiny bit. So when big chunks of hair started dropping to the floor, it was more than a little terrifying.

"Maybe this was a bad idea," she said.

Mystic held up a strand and clipped off another chunk. "A bad idea is going to bed with a man you don't even know."

"I know everything I need to know about Shane. He's got sizzling hot lips and talented fingers."

Mystic froze and stared at her in the mirror. "Talented fingers? Just how far did you two go?"

Delaney smirked. "Far enough to know he's a man who can please a woman."

"He gave you an orgasm?"

"Why do you think I'm in such a hurry for a repeat?"

Mystic continued cutting. "In my experience, men like to do the chasing. Maybe if you stopped chasing him, he'd start chasing you."

Delaney didn't know if she should be taking Mystic's advice. Mystic hadn't dated all that many men in her life. "But if I stop chasing him, I won't ever get what I want. He obviously has no problems avoiding me. He didn't even come down to breakfast this morning. I doubt he'll come down for dinner."

"Probably because he knew you'd be lying in wait. Maybe he's not as immune to you as you think and he's trying to keep his distance because you do tempt him." Mystic hesitated. "A person can only take so much temptation before they break."

"So how do I get him to hang out with me and be tempted if he won't come out of his room?"

Mystic lowered her scissors and tipped her head in thought. "What about if you needed his help with something?"

"Like what? I don't do computer stuff and he doesn't ranch. He can't even ride a horse."

Mystic's eyes widened. "The best cowgirl in the county's very first boyfriend can't ride a horse?" She laughed. "Now that's funny." She hesitated for a moment before she pointed her scissors at the mirror. "You could pretend to be injured. Men love to help out damsels in distress. You could act like you twisted your ankle and needed him to help you to your room."

"That would be great if I didn't live with overprotective siblings who would be all over me if I limped into the house. Shane wouldn't stand a chance of helping me even if he wanted to."

"You're right." Mystic went back to cutting. "That won't work. You need to get him away from everyone, where he's the only one who's there."

Before Delaney could ask how she could get Shane away from his beloved computer, Mystic set down the scissors and grabbed her blow-dryer. There was no talking above the racket. When Mystic finally finished styling her hair with the roller brush and whirled the chair around, Delaney was struck speechless.

"Well?" Mystic said.

Delaney stared at her hair that was now a good four inches shorter and as smooth as the highway blacktop that ran through town. "It looks . . ." She ran her hand over the straight strands. "Weird."

"You're just not used to it yet. Give it some time." Mystic took off the cape and shook it. "Take my word for it. Shane is going to love it. Now let's get some makeup on you."

When Mystic finished with the makeup, Delaney stared at her reflection in stunned silence. She didn't just look weird. She looked like someone completely different. Someone Delaney wouldn't want to be friends with. But maybe the perfectly coiffed woman staring back at her would be exactly the type of woman Shane would like.

"What happened to you?"

Delaney turned to see Hester standing in the doorway.

"I gave her a makeover," Mystic said. "Doesn't she look great?"

Hester walked in and let the door close behind

her. "Let me guess. You're trying to impress Shane." She sent Mystic a hard look. "I thought I taught you better, granddaughter. You never change who you are for a man."

"That advice hasn't exactly worked for me." Mystic fluffed Delaney's hair. "Besides, this makeover wasn't my idea."

Hester's eyes narrowed on Delaney. "Changing who you are to make other people happy is how you end up miserable. You should've learned this with your family. You've spent all your life trying to please them."

"Hessy!" Mystic said.

"Don't *Hessy* me. Delaney needs to hear this. I thought she'd learn it on her own, but it doesn't look like that's going to happen." Hester turned back to Delaney. "It's time you stopped trying to make everyone else happy and start trying to make yourself happy."

Delaney stared at her. "But what if I don't know what will make me happy?"

"I don't believe that for a second. You know what you want. You're just too scared to go after it."

"But that's what I'm doing. I want Shane and I'm going after him."

Hester looked taken back. "I thought you already had Shane."

Realizing her mistake, Delaney tried to backpedal. "Umm . . . well, I do. But . . . umm—"

Thankfully, Mystic helped her out. "But he wants to wait to have sex until they're married and Delaney doesn't want to wait. She's hoping to seduce him with her new makeover."

Hester hesitated for only a second before she took the purple crystal hanging around her neck in her hand and rubbed it. Her eyes grew dazed and kind of spooky before she released the stone and shook her head.

"A new haircut and makeup isn't going to work. I don't see a sexual relationship in Delaney's future at all."

Chapter Twelve

Delaney had finally given up on seducing him. There were no more knocks on the door late at night. No more heated caresses under the table at breakfast and dinner. In fact, she hadn't even called him "honey buns" once in the last two days.

Strangely, Shane missed it. He missed the teasing twinkle in her eyes when she used her term of endearment and slapped his butt. He missed the sexual tension he felt when her hand caressed his thigh or her breast brushed his arm. He even missed the taps on his door and her calling his name in a sexy whisper in the middle of the night.

She now completely ignored him during meals, instead focusing her attention on verbally sparing with Buck. He wasn't the only one who had noticed her coolness toward him. Yesterday, Stetson had called him into his office and asked if there was something going on between Shane and his sister. Shane had lied and said Delaney was just upset with him because he'd been so busy. Stetson hadn't looked like he believed him. And maybe that was a good thing. Stetson wouldn't be surprised when Delaney broke it off with him.

But Shane was confused why Stetson hadn't just asked Delaney what was going on. There seemed to be a huge communication problem between the elder Kingman and his younger siblings. Maybe it was because Stetson had taken the father role so early on. Whatever the reason, it annoyed Shane the way Stetson treated Delaney like a child and didn't value her opinions. There had been numerous times Shane had wanted to jump in and defend her ideas. If they had actually been engaged, he would have. But they weren't. He had no business getting involved in the Kingman family dynamic.

A knock sounded on the door. He couldn't help the smile that spread across his face. It looked like Delaney hadn't given up after all. Of course, he couldn't answer. Allowing Delaney into his room was the last thing he needed. Especially when he'd started to have dreams about her. Steamy sexual dreams of what would've happened if he hadn't rejected her in the tree house.

The knock came again, but it wasn't Delaney's voice that came through the door. It was Gretchen's.

"Shane, I hate to interrupt your work, but Miss Kitty says she needs to speak with you."

Sure enough, when Shane got downstairs, Kitty Carson was waiting in the foyer with her mailbag sitting at her feet and her buckteeth flashing in a smile.

"Hey, Shane! I have a special delivery package for you."

"Great." Shane waited for Kitty to take it out of her bag and hand it to him. Instead, she glanced at Gretchen who had followed him down the stairs.

"It's in the truck." Kitty waited until Shane followed her outside before she spoke again. "I really don't have a special package for you." She flung her mailbag into the truck. "I just didn't want anyone knowing that I'm helping you find the perfect ring. I got Delaney's ring size the other day at Mystic's." She pulled a ring out of the pocket of her khaki shorts and handed it to him. "This ring fit her perfect." She reached into her mailbag and pulled out a pile of junk mail. "And here's some engagement ring catalogs. They were supposed to go to Earl Sipes. But he ain't ever gonna get up the gumption to ask Ray Marie so I figure you can look through them before I deliver them to him."

Shane couldn't help but feel guilty that the woman had gone to so much trouble for his fake engagement. "Well, thank you, Miss Kitty."

"You're more than welcome. I like you, Shane Ransom. I've liked you ever since I met you." She winked at him. "Even though you tricked me with that twin switch. The fact that you're marryin' our little Delaney just fills my heart with joy. She needs a strong man to handle her feisty ways. The quicker you put a ring on that girl's finger, the better." She hopped into her mail truck. "Now I best be gettin' back to my route." With a wave, she zipped off.

Shane stood there for a moment, feeling like a complete jerk. Maybe it was time to call an end to the farce. No matter what Hester said, Chance seemed to be doing fine. Shane talked to him daily on the phone and had met him in town for breakfast on numerous occasions. While Chance still seemed to be grieving Lori, he didn't act like he had any problems with his faith. He talked about his sermons and the people in his congregation.

And Shane hadn't heard from Dan Fuller. So it was unlikely he was going to invest. It was time to end the fake engagement. Delaney's cold shoulder of late would give them the perfect excuse.

With his mind made up, Shane took the ring catalogs inside and grabbed his cowboy hat. When he got to the stables, he found Delaney in the paddock on the ugliest horse he'd ever seen. And the most talented. Or maybe the one with the talent was Delaney. She put the horse through a series of moves that had Shane awestruck. It was like watching two dancers perfectly in sync. Delaney's hands expertly held the reins and her toned thighs flexed with each lunge and dodge of the horse's body.

Shane was enthralled and impressed . . . and turned on. She glanced up and their gazes locked for a second or two before she looked away and finished the training routine. He thought she would continue to ignore him, but she finally walked the horse over to where he stood at the railing.

"So vampires do come out during the light of day."

Shane smiled. "I'm an anomaly." He stroked

the horse's forehead. "And so are you. No wonder you laughed when I said I'd never been on a ranch. You look like you were born in the saddle."

"I pretty much was. My mama loved horses. Stetson said she paid no attention to the doctors and continued to ride right up until Buck and I were born. Do you ride?"

"Not at all. But, according to my grandma, my daddy did." Once the words were out, he wanted them back. But it was too late.

"And he never taught you?"

He hesitated for a moment before he answered. "He didn't get a chance to. He had a problem with drugs and died before he even reached eighteen."

"Eighteen? How old were you and Chance when he passed?"

"Not even one."

"I'm sorry. What about your mama?"

"She still has a problem with drugs. Thankfully, she didn't want to take care of two babies and left us with Granny Ran."

"And you don't see her?"

"I tried once, but she wasn't receptive to meeting her sons."

He didn't know why he was being so honest. Maybe because Delaney had lived through her own losses and wasn't the type of woman to cry over a sob story. Her eyes only held understanding and empathy.

"I'm sorry. It's hard growing up without parents."

He shrugged. "We survived. And we were lucky

to have our grandma."

Delaney nodded. "I bet she was a strong woman."

"She was." He smiled at the memory of how strong his grandmother was. "You remind me a lot of her. Granny Ran was feisty and didn't have any problems going after what she wanted."

Delaney scowled. "I hope she had better luck than I have."

It was the perfect opening to discuss breaking their engagement. But before he could bring it up, Delaney's cellphone rang. She pulled it out of her pocket and answered.

"Delaney Kingman . . . oh, hey, Bud . . . they were just left in your cotton field . . . how many? . . . seven?" She hesitated. "Yeah, okay, I'll take them off your hands. See you in a few." She hung up and slipped her cellphone back in her pocket. "I have to go." She turned the horse and headed through the open doors of the stable.

Since Shane wanted to get the conversation about breaking up over with, he followed her. But once inside, he couldn't talk because a cowboy was there.

"I'll take care of getting Mutt unsaddled and cooled down, Del," the cowboy said as he took the reins from her.

"Thanks, Tab." Delaney dismounted and went to walk right by Shane.

He caught her arm. "We need to talk."

"You say that a lot, but I don't have time right now. Unless you want to come along and help me."

"Do what?"

"Pick up kids." She headed for the door and he followed.

"Kids?"

"Yeah, kids." She hopped into her truck that was parked outside. Curious, Shane hesitated for only a second before he opened the passenger door and got in. He figured it would give them a chance to talk. But he soon discovered it was hard to talk when Delaney Kingman was driving.

She drove fast, paying absolutely no attention to potholes or bumps . . . or even roads, for that matter. As soon as they left the ranch, she veered off onto a road that was more of a gully. As the truck bounced over rocks and deep ruts, talking was impossible. All Shane could do was hang on to the dashboard and hope the rocky ride would soon be over.

Delaney glanced over at him and grinned. "I guess you don't do much off-roadin'."

"Is that—what—this is—called?"

She laughed as she drove the truck into a deep ravine filled with mud. The tires spun, shooting mud everywhere, until they caught hold and the truck shot up the other side of the ravine and landed with a jarring bounce. After he got over his initial surprise, Shane laughed. Off-roading was damn fun. He continued to laugh as Delaney took him on the ride of his life, bouncing over rocks and dipping into muddy ravines and even splashing through a small stream. He was actually disappointed when they reached their destination. A large open warehouse half full of hay bales.

Delaney pulled around back where she expertly backed her truck up to a small trailer. She jumped out and Shane followed.

"What are you doing?" he asked.

"Hitching the trailer to put the kids in."

"I'm assuming we're talking about goats."

She laughed as she cranked the trailer lever that lowered the trailer hitch over the truck hitch. "Yes, pygmy goats. I wouldn't put seven kids in the back of a trailer."

"And you pick up other people's goats a lot?"

"People know I like goats so they call me when they find ones that have been abused or neglected. Or just left for dead."

"So you've already started your ranch for abused animals. Stetson just doesn't realize it."

Her smile took his breath away. "Smart man." She finished securing the trailer to the hitch and headed back to the truck.

With the trailer on the back, she drove more cautiously and stayed on the main roads.

"So what happened to these goats that you're picking up?" he asked.

"Bud Foster doesn't know. He just found them wandering around in his cotton field. Sometimes people think raising pygmy goats and selling them as pets will be a good way to make money and then realize goats are a lot more work and trouble than they thought."

"Could they have just wandered off on their own?"

"Doubtful. Kids usually don't stray too far from

their mamas."

"Did you say there was seven?"

She nodded. "Yep, seven."

Sure enough when they got to Bud Foster's farm, there were seven little goats waiting for them in Bud's barn. Delaney didn't hesitate to wade right into the middle of the mehhing group.

"She's something else with animals, ain't she?" Bud said as he and Shane watched her cuddle the kids and talk soothingly. "She's great with horses, can get a bull to eat right out of her hand, and has goats following her around like ducklings." Bud slapped him on the back. "You're one lucky man."

Bud turned out to be right. The kids did follow Delaney right out of the barn like little ducklings. With Bud's help, she had no problems getting them into the trailer. Except for the tiny white one with the three black stockings that flat refused to go into the trailer and kept running between Delaney's legs.

Finally, she gave up and scooped the goat into her arms. "Okay, little one, you don't have to go inside. You can sit up front." She handed the goat to Shane, who awkwardly held the kid away from him.

"Uhh . . . what do you want me to do with it?"

"Take it to the truck."

"And then what?"

Delaney stared at him for a second before she turned to Bud. "It looks like I got myself a greenhorn, Bud."

Bud laughed. "It does look that way." He

thumped Shane on the back again. "But he'll learn. Especially when he has such a good teacher."

Delaney shot Shane a glance. "It's too bad he's not willing to teach me what he knows."

Shane knew exactly what she wanted him to teach her. Although the answer was a firm no, he couldn't stop the zing of desire that shot through him at just the thought of becoming Delaney's sex teacher.

He turned away and carried the goat to the truck. When Bud and Delaney were finished securing the other kids, she joined him. She smiled at the goat sleeping in Shane's arms.

"See, Dopey didn't bite."

"Dopey?"

She started the truck and waved at Bud before she headed out of the long drive. "I thought since there's seven of them I'd name them after the dwarfs. He's the smallest so he should be Dopey." She reached over and petted his head. "And he's just as cute."

Shane had to agree. The baby pygmy goat was pretty cute. He stroked his back and glanced over at Delaney. "I think we should break our engagement."

She didn't say anything for a long moment, then she finally spoke. "I guess Hester was right. We're not going to have sex."

"You asked Hester about sex?"

"I wanted to know if I had a chance or was wasting my time." That explained why she had given up trying to get him in bed.

He sighed. "It would've been a mistake, Del."

She didn't reply. "So how do you want to do it? A huge fight or do you want to just leave?"

"I'm not going to slink off in the middle of the night." Like his mother had. "We'll talk to your family and my brother together. We'll say it's a mutual decision. We just weren't compatible."

She glanced over at him. "I think we would've been compatible in bed."

It was hard to look away from the desire he read in her pretty blue eyes—the same desire that raced through him. They *would've* been compatible in bed. It was too damn bad his conscience wouldn't let him.

When they got to the ranch, Shane set Dopey on the ground so he could help Delaney lower the trailer door. The baby goats trotted down the ramp and started to investigate their new home. That's when Stetson showed up.

"What the hell is this, Del?"

Delaney smiled brightly. "These are my new kids." She pointed at the goats. "Doc, Sleepy, Sneezy, Bashful, Happy, and that one hiding behind Shane's legs is Dopey. Oh, and Grumpy. Although, by the look on your face, that name should be reserved for you."

"Damn right I'm grumpy. What did I tell you about bringing home more goats?"

"I couldn't just let Bud call animal services. They won't know how to care for baby goats. Or have the time to do it right."

"And you have the time? You know I count on you to manage the horse breeding and training.

When are you going to have time to take care of a bunch of orphaned kids?"

Shane didn't know what came over him. One second, he was standing there minding his own business, and the next second, he was saying something he had no business saying.

"I'll help."

Stetson turned to him with surprise. "You know about goats?"

"No, but I'm a fast learner. If Delaney tells me what to do, I can do it."

Shane didn't know who looked more shocked. Stetson or Delaney. She had a right to be. He had just told her that he wanted to break their fake engagement and now he wanted to stay on the ranch and help her take care of goats? Had he lost his mind?

Stetson stared at him for a moment more before he looked back at Delaney. "That's not the point. I told you no more goats, Del."

Again, Shane found himself butting in. "Why not? Do pygmy goats cause problems for horses and cattle? I mean, this is Delaney's ranch too, right? So why can't she rescue goats if she wants to? Rescuing animals would be good for Kingman Ranch's image."

"What's going on?" Buck walked out of the stables. When he saw the goats running playfully around the stable yard, his eyes widened. "Hell, no! Do not tell me Delaney brought home more goats." He looked at Stetson. "You're not going to go along with this, are you, Stet?"

Stetson hesitated for a moment before he

turned to Delaney. "Make sure they don't run around the ranch like that other goat of yours." He turned and walked off.

Buck called after him. "That's it? Come on, Stet. If you let her get away with this, we'll soon be a goat ranch."

"We'll never be a goat ranch, little brother." Delaney socked Buck playfully in the arm. "So stop worrying. I'm sure I can find someone who will adopt these cuties once they get weaned."

"And until then? Who's going to help you take care of them? Because if you think I am, you've got another think coming."

She looked at Shane. "My fiancé has volunteered." She leaned over and kissed his cheek. "Thank you."

It was just a simple kiss. And yet, the spot her lips touched tingled with a warmth that spread through Shane's entire body. When she drew back, her blue eyes sparkled teasingly as she smacked him on the butt.

"Come on, honey buns. Let's introduce our kids to their new home."

Chapter Thirteen

If anyone had asked Delaney if she was happy with her life, she would've answered in the affirmative without hesitation. Despite her battles with Buck and her disagreements with Stetson, she loved her family and the ranch where she'd grown up with all her heart.

But in the week that followed, she'd discovered that there were different levels of happiness. There was the happiness of ranching and being surrounded by a loving family . . . and then there was the giddy kind of happiness you couldn't explain.

At least, Delaney couldn't explain it. She didn't know why she woke up with an excited feeling in the pit of her stomach. Or why she went to bed each night with a feeling of warm contentment. She didn't know why she caught herself smiling for no reason. Or why even cloudy days seemed sunny.

It had to be the baby goats. The seven kids had a way of making everyone happy. They'd become the ranch's main attraction. The entire family, including Stetson, stopped by the barn to watch their antics. But Delaney's favorite time with the goats was feeding time.

Three times a day, she and Shane would meet up in the barn to feed the kids. Delaney had tried to get some of the mama goats who had recently birthed their own kids to surrogate the orphan pygmies, but with no luck. It took her and Shane a good hour to bottle-feed all seven goats. With nothing else to do while the kids suckled, she and Shane talked.

They talked about everything. Their favorite college courses and the ones they hated. Shane's ideas for apps and Delaney's ideas on helping abused and neglected animals. What it was like growing up in a huge castle and what it was like growing up in a two-bedroom trailer.

They had a lot of differences. But, surprisingly, there were quite a few similarities. They loved Mexican food and hated asparagus. They believed in God and occasionally felt guilty that they didn't attend church more. They had both lost their parents at early ages and had been raised by other family members—loving, but strict, family members who taught them to mind their manners and do their chores.

"The chore I hated most was collecting the eggs from the henhouse," Delaney said as she held the bottles for the female goats, Happy and Bashful. "We had a mean old hen who was extremely protective of her eggs and she'd peck me every single time and draw blood."

"You're kidding." Shane stared at her in disbelief as he fed Doc and Grumpy. "There was an animal on this ranch who didn't like Delaney Dolittle?"

"Just one. And Charlotte was a mean ol' biddy."

Shane laughed. "My worst chore was ironing. My grandmother took in laundry to supplement her social security. I can't tell you how many hours I spent at an ironing board."

Delaney glanced at his wrinkled western shirt. "Ahh, that explains it."

Shane shrugged. "I swore when I left home that I'd never lift another iron again."

"So I guess when we get married, I'll have to do the ironing." They had started teasing each other about their fake married life.

Shane flashed a grin. "Of course, But don't worry, sugar pea, I'll be more than happy to feed our kids." He adjusted the bottles he held. "I'm getting damn good at this."

He had gotten damn good at it. After only a few days, he handled the goats as well as she did. He even came out to the pasture to meet the other goats and took a turn at trying to milk. But he refused to get on a horse to get to the goat pasture.

"I prefer four wheels to four legs."

Delaney shook her head as she climbed into his beat-up truck. "I don't know how I said 'yes' to a man who doesn't even know how to ride."

"Like I said before, I know how to ride."

Delaney didn't laugh. Sex was the one joke she didn't find funny. Shane wanted her. She knew he wanted her. She saw it in his warm brown eyes every time she caught him looking at her.

She felt it in the tremble of his body whenever their hands accidentally touched—or not so accidentally. But Delaney believed Hester. Shane was never going to give in and have sex with her. There would be no more hot kisses. No more mind-blowing orgasms.

It was frustrating. Just not frustrating enough to dampen her giddy happiness. Which was weird. How could she be so happy when she wasn't even getting any sex?

It had to be the goats.

On Friday, when she stepped into the barn to feed the kids, she couldn't help whistling "Whistle While You Work."

"Those goats have screwed with your head, Del."

She startled and turned to see Buck coming out of a stall with a pitchfork. "Dang, Buck. Don't sneak up on people like that. You nearly gave me a heart attack. What are you doing in the barn? I thought you were starting spring branding."

He shrugged, and for the first time, she noticed how sad he looked. "I didn't feel like branding today."

"What's wrong?"

"Nothing's wrong."

She bumped his shoulder with hers. "Liar. We might not be the kind of twins who read each other's minds, but I know when you're unhappy. What's going on? Is Mystic spending too much time at the salon and not enough time here at the ranch? You always get grumpy when you don't get to see her."

"It's not that. It's just . . ." He sighed. "Everyone is getting married and having kids."

So that was it. Delaney should've known. Buck had wanted to fall in love and get married since graduating from high school. She didn't know why her little brother had always been so set on getting married—especially when their parents hadn't exactly had a perfect marriage. Their father had married their mother for her ranch and ended up breaking her heart with his numerous affairs.

Maybe that was it. Buck wanted to have what his parents hadn't.

Delaney couldn't help feeling guilty about her hoax. "Shane and I aren't married yet. You could find your one true love and beat us to the altar."

He snorted. "That's doubtful. I've been looking for her for years and haven't found her yet."

She playfully socked him in the arm. "Maybe she's right in front of your face and you're just too stupid to see her. You can be pretty dumb." When he didn't laugh at her teasing, she put an arm around his neck and tugged him close. "You'll find her, Buck. I know you will. In the meantime, you can practice being a daddy by helping me feed the kids."

It turned out Buck didn't dislike goats as much as he let on. Dopey seemed to be one of his favorites. Although it was hard not to love the runt. He was always getting into something. Buck and Delaney both laughed when he got his head stuck in an empty feed bucket.

They were still laughing when Shane appeared

in the open door of the stall. He usually wore wrinkled western shirts, but today he wore a faded blue T-shirt that hugged his biceps and the curves of his chest. She couldn't see his eyes in the shadow of his straw hat, but she could feel his gaze. As always, it left her feeling warm and breathless . . . and happy.

When he greeted her with a deep, gravelly, "Good mornin'," the feelings intensified. She wished she had taken the time that morning to fix her hair or put on a little makeup.

"Good mornin'," she said as she got to her feet and dusted the straw off her butt. "You're a little late for our kids' morning feeding, Daddy. Their Uncle Buck already helped me."

He flashed a smile. He had a nice smile—soft at the corners with just a touch of white, even teeth. "Sorry, sugar pea. But I need to go into town this morning."

"You're going to town?" She took the bucket off Dopey's head. "What for?"

"I'm meeting a college friend for breakfast at Good Eats and then Mystic is cutting my hair."

Buck jumped to his feet and he and Delaney spoke at the same time. "Mystic's cutting your hair?"

Shane glanced between them. "Umm . . . yeah. Is something wrong with that?"

Delaney didn't know what the feeling was that reared up inside her. All she knew was that she didn't want Mystic Malone running her fingers through Shane's hair. Especially when Delaney didn't get to do it.

"Mystic doesn't cut men's hair," she said. "Only women's."

"But she said she cuts Buck's hair."

"Only because we're friends," Buck said. "And I don't have the heart to tell her that she can't cut men's hair worth a flip." He pulled out his cellphone. "Joe Simpson is a damn fine barber who cuts hair in his garage. I'll call him. I'm sure he can get you in this morning."

"That's okay. I wouldn't want to break my appointment with Mystic on such short notice. I'm not worried about her messing up my hair." Shane tipped his hat. "See y'all later."

Delaney stood there for a second, not sure what to do, when Buck spoke. "There's something I need in town."

"Me too!" she said.

They both headed for the stall door at the same time and got into a bit of a shoving contest before they made it through. By the time they got to the house, Shane's beat-up truck was heading down the road to town. They hopped into Buck's green monster truck that he called Frog and followed. Or not followed. Buck took an off-road shortcut.

"Why are you in such an all-fired hurry to get to town?" Delaney asked as she held on to the dashboard. "I thought you and Mystic were just friends."

"We are. This isn't about me. I just don't want my little sister's heart broken if she loses her fiancé to Mystic's magic fingers."

"So this doesn't have a thing to do with you being jealous of Mystic touching another man's hair?"

His hands tightened on the steering wheel as he gunned the truck through a mud puddle. "Not a damn thing."

When they reached Cursed, Buck pulled into the parking lot of Good Eats. They must've beaten Shane into town because his truck was nowhere to be seen.

"You try to keep Shane here for as long as you can," Buck said. "I'll head over to the Cut and Curl to see if I can figure out a way to get Mystic to cancel his appointment."

"And just what reason am I going to give him for coming to town?"

"You're his fiancée. Just say you missed him and wanted to spend the day with him."

Since she couldn't argue without telling him about the fake engagement, she nodded and hopped out.

Good Eats might not look like much on the outside with its crumbling stucco and faded sign. But on the inside, it looked and smelled like a country diner. The linoleum floor was spotless, the gingham tablecloths and curtains cheerful, and the bacon-and-coffee scent divine. The restaurant was owned and run by Otis and Thelma Davenport. When Delaney stepped in the door, she was greeted by both. Otis waved his spatula from the kitchen with a, "Hey, Del," while Thelma hurried over with a coffeepot in her hand.

"Hey there, Delaney! What brings you into town this early?"

"Uhh . . . I'm meeting Shane for breakfast."

Thelma looked confused. "But doesn't Shane live with you?"

Before she could come up with an excuse for meeting Shane at the diner, a woman's voice cut in.

"Shane lives with you?"

Delaney turned to the woman who sat on a stool at the counter. She was model thin with multicolored hair that went from magenta red at the roots to platinum blond on the tips. She wore zebra-striped yoga pants that hugged her curvy butt and long legs and a low-cut black tank top that showed plenty of cleavage and the tattoo on the curve of one breast. Her cat-angled hazel eyes studied Delaney with an intent look.

"You live with Shane Ransom?"

Delaney nodded. "Do you know Shane?"

The woman didn't answer, but, for one split second, a look passed over her beautiful features that could only be described as intense pain. She recovered quickly and pinned on a smile.

"Well, I'll be damned. Shaney finally found someone to put up with him." She stood and held out a hand. "Everly Grayson. I'm an old college friend of Shane's."

Before Delaney could get over her surprise, the door opened and Shane stepped in. He looked surprised to see Delaney, but his surprise was eclipsed by joy when he saw Everly.

"Ev!" He strode over and swept her up in his arms.

Delaney had never understood why women fought over men, but she understood it now. Talk about the green-eyed monster. She had a strong desire to get in an out-and-out catfight with the woman who had her arms looped around Shane's neck and her full lips pressed to his cheek.

This was the friend Shane was meeting for breakfast? Delaney had assumed it was a guy. She hadn't assumed it was a stunningly beautiful woman who didn't look at Shane like he was just a friend.

Suddenly, Delaney didn't feel so happy. In fact, she felt very unhappy. And sick to her stomach.

Shane turned to her with confusion in her eyes. "What are you doing here, Delaney? I just left you at the ranch."

Before Delaney had to answer, Everly spoke. "I thought you were just hanging out in this Podunk town to make sure Chance was okay. You didn't mention that you'd met a woman and were living with her."

"That's love for you," Thelma said with a big smile. "One second, you're single and free, and the next, you're engaged to get married."

"Married?" Everly stared at Shane. If there had been any questions about their relationship, they were answered by Shane's guilty look.

Suddenly, Delaney felt like a complete fool. No wonder he didn't want to have sex with her. Why would he have sex with her when he had women who looked like Everly waiting with open arms? While Delaney had been mooning over him like a starstruck teenager, he'd just been killing time until they could break off the engagement without causing problems for his brother. Shane had worried about her developing feelings for him if they had sex and she'd laughed as if that was the silliest notion. But they hadn't even had sex and she had developed feelings for him.

How pathetic was that?

What was even more pathetic was that she'd let Shane see her hurt. His eyes held concern as he took her arm. "If you'll excuse us, I need to talk to Delaney." When they got outside, he turned to her. "It's not what you think, Del. Everly is not my girlfriend."

Delaney had two choices. She could let him know he'd been right and she'd fallen for him. Or she could bluff her way through. Bluffing had always been her forte.

"I don't care if she is your girlfriend. It's not like we're actually engaged, Shane. I was just surprised, is all. But it's a good thing Everly showed up. I think it made us both realize that it's time to call an end to this farce. You don't belong with a goat-luvin' country girl." She forced a smile. "And I sure don't belong with a city boy who doesn't even know how to ride a horse."

Chapter Fourteen

"When I came to this town, I expected to have a little more excitement than watching two brothers shoot hoops in a parsonage driveway." Everly rebounded the basketball Shane had just unsuccessfully shot at the basket and threw it back to him. "I mean Cursed sounded like my kind of town—an unholy den of iniquity." She glanced at Chance. "No offense, Preach."

But if Chance's scowl was any indication, he'd taken offense. Of course, he always seemed to take offense to Everly. From the time Shane had first introduced them in college, Chance had never liked her. She was a little too wild and outspoken for his brother's taste.

Which was exactly why Shane loved her so much. Although he could've done without her showing up unexpectedly. No matter what Delaney had said, he knew Everly was behind Delaney's sudden need to break their fake engagement. It had been easy to read the hurt in her eyes. It was her hurt that kept Shane from trying to talk her out of ending their relationship. If Delaney got upset just because an old friend showed up, then it *was* time to end things between them.

The knot in Shane's gut confirmed it.

He'd gotten attached too. He'd gotten used to sitting in a pile of hay with Delaney and talking while they fed the goats. He'd gotten used to her laughter. He'd gotten used to her teasing. He'd gotten used to . . . her.

It wasn't just Delaney he'd gotten used to. He'd also gotten used to large family meals filled with laughter and arguments. And to the mooing, neighing, mehhing sounds that greeted him when he walked to the stables and barn. Delaney had only broken things off that morning, but Shane already missed the ranch.

"Are you going to shoot or stand there staring at the basket?" Everly asked. Shane pulled out of his thoughts and took the shot. The ball went completely over the backboard.

Everly rolled her eyes and threw up her hands. "Well, that's enough of this shit show. I'm going to go find the bar and get drunk. And don't tell me this town doesn't have one. Every small town in Texas has a bar. My hometown has two. One for the Protestants with a dance floor and one for the Baptists without." She winked at Chance. "Again, no offense, Preach." She walked over and kissed Shane on the cheek. "Come join me when you're through playing games, Shaney." She started going in the wrong direction and Shane grabbed her arm and turned her around.

"Nasty Jack's is that way."

"Ohh, Nasty Jack's. Sounds like my kind of place." She headed down the street with a saucy strut that made Shane smile.

"She's still in love with you."

Shane glanced at Chance who had retrieved the basketball and was bouncing it back and forth between his hands. Shane sighed. "I know."

"And you think it's wise to continue your friendship?"

"Probably not. But Everly isn't a woman who lets go easily."

"And Delaney? You think she'll let go easily?"

After Delaney had broken it off, Shane had confessed all to his brother and Everly. Everly had found the fake engagement amusing. Chance not so much.

"She isn't in love with me. Just slightly infatuated." Shane held his hands out for the ball. When Chance threw it to him, he went up for a jump shot. He missed again. He was obviously having a bad night.

Chance rebounded, took a shot, and the ball hit nothing but net before bouncing to the concrete driveway below. They had both played basketball in high school, but Chance had always been twice as good as Shane. Shane had been too busy trying to come up with his next get-rich-quick scheme to spend time practicing.

They continued to play—Chance hitting and Shane missing—until one of Shane's wayward shots had the ball going over the neighbor's side fence. They stood there for a moment looking at the high fence before Chance spoke.

"For a broken fake engagement, you're certainly acting like it was real."

Shane released his breath and ran a hand through his hair. "Stupid, right?"

Chance shrugged. "Why is it stupid to like Delaney?"

"Because we're too different. She's a rich cowgirl who lives on a ranch and I'm a poor software developer who lives in the city. You see what happened with Everly. I don't want to hurt another woman."

"It looks like it's a little too late to worry about that. It sounds like Delaney was already hurt." Chance studied him. "And I think you are too."

He wanted to deny it, but he couldn't. "Okay, so I'm feeling a little screwed up over ending things with Delaney, but it's for the best. I can't let a woman distract me from my goals."

"Like Mama distracted Daddy?"

Shane didn't reply. He and Chance had both been affected by what had happened to their parents—even though they hadn't been there to witness their parents' implosion. Granny Ran had told them the details when they got old enough to understand.

James Ransom had been voted the most likely to succeed in high school. He'd been the poorest kid in town, but he'd also been the most driven. He'd been an excellent student, a star athlete, and a hard worker who helped out his widowed mother by working odd jobs around town . . . until he'd hooked up with Jessie White. Jessie was beautiful and charming and popular—no doubt because she sold the crystal meth her brothers cooked in their garage.

According to Granny Ran, Jessie had gotten James to start taking meth. Jessie had changed James from an honor student who was headed for college to a druggie who got her pregnant and then died before his sons could even walk.

"Delaney isn't Jessie," Chance cut into his thoughts. "And you're not James. In fact, we don't even know if Granny Ran's story was accurate. James was Granny's son. She couldn't see him as the bad boy. Only as the golden boy who had been led astray."

"I know," Shane said. "But it's still a lesson to learn from. I can't get distracted from my goals. I need to stay focused."

"Maybe you're too focused on making money. All you do in Dallas is stay holed up in your apartment, working on your computer and eating delivery food. You never answer my calls or texts. But the last few weeks, you've been different. You've been happier and more relaxed."

"And I haven't gotten much work done."

"Who cares? Happiness is more important than money."

Shane snorted. "You sound like Hester Malone."

"You let Hester tell your fortune?"

"You don't let Hester do anything. She just does it." He hesitated. "She also mentioned you. She said you're struggling with your faith. Are you, Chance?"

Chance sighed and stared up at the night sky. "Lately, I've had my doubts."

"Why didn't you say something? I wouldn't have pushed you to take the job here if I'd known. I wouldn't have butted my nose in where it didn't belong."

Chance looked at Shane and grinned. "Yes, you would've. That's what brothers do. Why do you think I'm out here shooting hoops when I have a sermon to write? I wanted to offer you some sound brotherly advice." His smile faded. "I want you to be happy, Shane. Just like you want me to be. Even if it was a hoax, I think Delaney made you happy. I think she still can. I get that you have financial goals you want to meet. But don't let money goals get in the way of finding personal happiness."

Shane sighed. "Let me guess. Money is the root of all evil."

"Actually, the Bible doesn't say that. It says, 'the love of money is the root of all evil.' Don't put it before love of people. Now, enough of my brotherly advice. Let's shoot some hoops." Chance glanced at the neighbor's fence. "And since you're the one responsible, you're the one who needs to go get it."

There was a good reason Chance sent him after the ball. Shane barely escaped the neighbor's Doberman. After Shane made it back over the wall by the skin of his butt and Chance had a good laugh at his expense, they played a game of HORSE. Shane lost badly. When Chance got his final *E*, Shane rebounded and tossed him the ball.

"I better go check on Everly."

"I think she's the type of woman who can take

care of herself. You should check on Delaney instead."

"I'll have to pass on that, little bro." Shane headed down the street.

Since it was Saturday night, Nasty Jack's was packed. Shane had to push his way through a log-jam of cowboys and cowgirls to get to the bar. Wolfe was bartending. Shane expected the usual scowl. Instead, Wolfe had a look that was almost kind as he filled a glass with beer and set it on a cocktail napkin in front of Shane.

"Del says she broke it off with you." Wolfe studied him. "She says you're too much of a city boy. She said you can't even ride a horse."

Shane shrugged. "I can't."

Wolfe stared at him for a long uncomfortable moment before he spoke. "So learn." He turned and headed down the bar to take the orders from a couple cowgirls while Shane sat there feeling stunned. Had Wolfe just given Shane his blessing to try and win Delaney back? And why did the idea of winning her back hold so much appeal? Delaney was right. They didn't belong together. He needed to accept that and move on.

He stood on the rungs of the barstool and looked over the sea of cowboy hats, trying to find Everly so they could leave. He didn't find Everly, but Kitty Carson found him.

"Shane!" She pushed her way through the crowd to get to him. "I'm so glad you're here. Did you get a chance to look at those catalogs?"

For some reason, he *had* looked through the catalogs. Why, he didn't know.

"Yes, I looked through them. But not one is right for Delaney. She wouldn't want a flashy engagement ring. It's just not her style. She'd want something simple and meaningful. But the ring doesn't matter anymore. Delaney and I broke off our engagement."

Kitty sighed. "That's what I was afraid of. Thelma told me all about your ex-girlfriend showing up at the diner. I figure that's why Delaney's out on the dance floor right now with that randy ranch hand."

Shane stared at her. "She's on the dance floor with a randy ranch hand?"

"She sure is. They're as cuddled up as too bugs in a—"

He didn't wait for her to finish before he pushed his way through the crowd. Sure enough, when he got to the dance floor, he discovered Delaney in the arms of a cowboy Shane had seen working around the ranch. If she was upset over their breakup, she wasn't showing it. Her head was tipped back in laughter as the cowboy swirled her around the floor.

Jealousy was too mild a word for the feeling that punched Shane hard in the chest. It more than surprised him. He had been jealous of people who struck it rich, but never of women. And yet, there he was fighting the strong desire to break every one of the man's fingers that were resting on Delaney's waist.

Without any thought, he stepped onto the dance floor and moved toward the laughing couple. When he reached them, he tapped the cowboy on the shoulder. "I believe this is my dance."

The cowboy started to step away, but Delaney jerked him back. "Sorry, but this dance is already taken." She led the man away. With nothing else to do, Shane left the dance floor. But he didn't go far. He stood there with his arms crossed and his insides rolling with anger as Delaney swept past time and time again.

"Oooh, it looks like Shaney has a temper after all."

Shane glanced over to see Everly standing there looking completely out of place in her zebra yoga pants and hot-pink running shoes. A large cowboy was standing right behind her with his hand on her back. She turned and winked at him.

"Would you go get me a lemon drop martini, sweetie?"

"A what?"

Everly sighed. "Just make it a Corona with a squeeze of lime." When he was gone, she looked back at Shane. "I guess your feelings run a little deeper than you thought."

"I just don't want someone taking advantage of her."

Everly laughed. "You mean you don't want someone getting what you want."

Shane might have disagreed if he hadn't lost sight of Delaney. When he glanced around, he saw her and the cowboy heading out the back door. "Shit!" He walked straight across the dance floor, dodging around waltzing couples, to follow them.

Once outside, he searched through the sea of mud-splattered trucks until he found Delaney's. She was standing by it. Or not standing by it as much as pressed up against it by the ranch hand. As Shane watched, she pulled the cowboy's head down for a kiss.

The jealousy Shane had felt before was nothing compared to the surge of rage that flooded his body. There was only one thought in his mind.

Get the man's lips off his sugar pea.

Chapter Fifteen

Delaney had hoped Boomer's kiss would wipe all thoughts of Shane out of her head and set her world to rights. It didn't. Instead, the entire time she was kissing Boomer, Delaney was comparing the kiss to Shane's. It fell short. Far short. She was about to pull away when Boomer was jerked from her by an extremely angry-looking computer nerd.

"Stay the fuck away from her!" Shane shoved Boomer back against the truck. When he lifted his fist, Delaney finally snapped out of her shock and jumped in between them.

"What the hell is wrong with you?"

Shane blinked a few times as if to clear his vision before his arm lowered. "What the hell is wrong with me? What the hell is wrong with you? We haven't even been broken up for one day and you're kissing another man?"

"Hey, dude." Boomer moved from behind her. "It wasn't my idea."

Shane snorted and continued to glare at Delaney. "Of course it wasn't. Now get the hell out of here."

Boomer hurried off.

When he was gone, Shane stepped back from Delaney and held up his hands. "So that's it? You're now just going to give your virginity to any cowboy?"

"And what business is that of yours? You didn't want it."

He stared at her for a long moment before he turned and walked away. "Grow up, Delaney."

She chased after him. "Grow up? You're the one who needs to grow up. You can't have sex with me without having all kinds of rules and regulations, but I'm sure you had no problem having sex with Everly without any rules."

He kept walking. "I didn't pick up Everly in a bar parking lot."

The fact that he didn't deny having sex with Everly made Delaney livid. "So if you hadn't met me in a bar parking lot, you would've had sex with me? And for your information, I wasn't going to have sex with Boomer. If I had sex with just any cowboy, I would've had sex a long time ago. As much as my brothers watch over me, I've had opportunities."

He stopped and turned to her. "So the entire 'Woe is me, my brothers keep me locked in a tower' routine was just you playing the part of a Kingman spoiled princess."

She stomped her foot. "I'm not a spoiled princess!"

"You're right. You're not a princess. You work your ass off for the family business. But you're still a sheltered woman who is terrified of growing up. You act like you're so tough. Delaney Kingman who can ride, rope, and ranch better than any man. And you can. But what you can't do is stand up to your overprotective family and take charge of your life."

Delaney wanted to tell him he was wrong. Dead wrong. But she couldn't speak with the lump in the back of her throat. All she could do was stand there and absorb the truth. She turned and headed back to her truck. But he wouldn't let her leave with a trace of dignity. He grabbed her arm and spun her around.

"Why me? If you had other opportunities to have sex? Why did you choose me?" When she didn't answer, he took her other arm and shook her. "Why, Delaney?"

Her eyes burned with tears. "Because I knew I could trust you!" she blurted out.

He released her and stared at her with confused eyes. "But you didn't even know me."

She blinked away the tears before they could fall. "I didn't have to know you. I've always had good instincts with animals. I know when a horse will take me on a nice, gentle walk or try and buck me off. Or if a dog is going to greet me with licks or aggression. I knew you wouldn't hurt me. Maybe it was the way you got after that trucker for cussing in front of me. Or the way you smiled when I beat you at pool—like you weren't mad, just impressed. Or the way you asked permission to kiss me when I was the one who followed you out to the parking lot. Even when things got hot and heavy, you allowed me to take the lead. I knew all I had to do to get you to stop was ask."

He released his breath in a heavy sigh. "That's still all you have to do. After you broke our engagement, I had no right to interfere tonight. You've made your choice." His eyes held hurt—a whole lot of hurt—before he turned and walked away.

She should've let him go. Whatever she felt for Shane had become too intense and scary. But then his words came back to her. She realized he was right. She was a woman too scared to grow up. She had blamed her brothers for keeping men away from her, but deep down she had found security in their protection and had used it as an excuse to not take responsibility for her own life decisions. It was much easier to blame her inexperience on her brothers, than to blame herself for being too scared to take charge of her own life. Yes, caring about someone was scary. But letting them walk out of your life was even scarier.

"Sha-ne!" Her voice cracked, betraying all the emotion she had been trying so hard to keep in.

He froze, his body tight and his fists clenched. He turned and his gaze locked with hers. They stared at each for what felt like forever before he retraced his steps in long strides and pulled her into his arms. His kiss was everything she had been looking for in Boomer's kiss. Consuming, enflaming . . . healing.

She wrapped her arms around his neck and gave herself up to him because she did trust him.

She didn't know how long they kissed. When he finally drew back, her legs were hiked around his waist, his hands firmly cupping her butt.

"What do you want, Delaney?" he asked in a husky voice.

She didn't even have to think. "You."

He gave a brief nod before he carried her to her truck. He leaned her against the side as he opened the door. Then he gently deposited her into the passenger seat and held out his hand. "Since you've probably been drinking, I'll drive."

She hadn't been drinking, but his kisses had left her feeling drunk. Without argument, she fished the keys out of her pocket and handed them to him. He gave her one more heated kiss as he buckled her in, then he drew back and slammed the door.

They drove in silence to the ranch. It wasn't until they passed under the Kingman Ranch entrance sign that she turned to him. "Just so I'm clear. What are we doing?"

He glanced over at her. "What do you want to do?"

"I think I've made it very clear what I want to do."

He returned his gaze to the road and it took him a long time to answer. "I want to do that too."

"And what about the entire first time needs to be special thing?"

He sighed. "I've decided I'm willing to take on the responsibility of making your first time special." He paused. "As long as you realize that I'm going back to Dallas."

She knew that. She also knew it would be hard

to let him go. But Boomer's kiss had made her realize that what she had with Shane might never happen again. As scared as she was of getting hurt, she couldn't pass up a chance to experience at least one night in his arms. She didn't know what would happen in the morning. She didn't know if he would leave and she'd never see him again. She didn't know if he would stay and they would enjoy each other for as long as they could. All she knew was she wanted Shane to be her first.

When he started to drive around the house, she stopped him. "What are you doing?"

"I thought we'd go to the tree house."

She shook her head. "The tree house was a childish idea. Kingman castle is my home. I can bring my ex-fiancé back to my room if I want to."

Although when they got inside and ran into Stetson coming out of the great room, Delaney didn't feel quite so cocky. Stetson's approval had always meant so much to her. It still did. But it was time to make her own choices.

"Hey, Stet," she said. "As you can see, Shane and I made up. So . . . we'll see you in the morning." She pulled Shane up the stairs. Halfway up, he scooped her into his arms. She had always thought women allowing men to carry them was weak and stupid. But she didn't feel that way now. Being in Shane's arms made her feel special. She released a very girlie giggle.

"What are you doing?"

"I'm trying to be a gallant hero. I want this night to be a night you don't forget." He stumbled on the top stair and she tightened her arms around his neck.

"If you drop me down these stairs, I'm sure I won't forget it."

But he didn't drop her. They made it all the way to his room without another misstep. She helped him open the door and he carried her inside and kicked it closed.

He set her down by the bed and drew her in for a kiss. He took his time, his lips performing a slow seductive dance that left Delaney feeling as woozy as if she'd downed an entire bottle of tequila. As he seduced her with his mouth, his hands divested her of her clothes. Before she knew it, her shirt and bra had slipped to the floor and his hands were caressing her bare skin—stroking her spine, gliding along her arms and shoulders, testing the width of her waist . . . and finally cradling her breast.

He didn't squeeze, he merely held it softly as her heart beat crazily against his palm. Then he brushed her nipple with his thumb in a slow, unhurried, back-and-forth motion until she was mindless with desire. He did the same to her other breast while he continued to hypnotize her with his slow, drugging kisses.

When both her nipples were tight and achy, he drew back from the kiss and dipped his head to take one in his mouth. The sweet suction had her burrowing her fingers through his hair and moaning. It was like a live electrical wire ran from her nipple to the spot between her legs. Every time his lips tugged and his tongue brushed, a zap of heat singed her there, turning Delaney into a quivering mass of need.

"Shane," she moaned. "Please."

He lifted his head and kissed her again, speaking against her lips. "I love to hear you beg. And I promise I'm going to give you everything you're begging for, Del." He slipped the button of her jeans free and slid down her zipper, then drew back from the kiss to push her jeans and panties past her hips. Just the brush of the fabric against her aching need was enough to have her knees buckling.

"Easy, baby." He settled a firm hand on her bare butt cheek and steadied her. "I got you."

Then he touched her, his fingers slipping between her legs and into her wet heat. It only took a few strokes for her to reach orgasm. Her body tensed and her head fell back as she thrust her hips closer to the experienced fingers that carried her over the edge. He slowed his strokes and wrung out every last shiver of ecstasy from her body. When her knees gave out completely, he picked her up in his arms and laid her on the bed. She heard the soft thump of her cowboy boots hitting the floor and leaned up on her elbows.

"You stole my boot."

His hands froze as he was pulling off her jeans and panties. "I didn't steal it. You left it in my truck. So technically, it's mine."

"You still have it?"

"Yes, Cinderella. I still have it."

She felt all giddy inside. "Why?"

He finished pulling her clothes off, then quickly removed his. She wished there was more light in the room. She wanted to see every inch of his naked body. Although when he joined her on the bed, she got to feel it. The heat of his skin. The bunch and flex of his muscles. And the hard, prodding length of his erection.

A tingle of desire raced through her. More tingles followed when he slid his arm around her waist and kissed his way along her neck. When he finally answered her question, his voice fell low and breathy against her ear.

"Because I didn't want to forget you. But you're impossible to forget, Delaney Kingman." He nipped her ear with his teeth, sending a shockwave through her. "I'm going to make sure you don't ever forget me."

There was no way she would forget him. Even if he stopped right then.

But he didn't.

He continued to set her body on fire with heated caresses that started at her breasts and then moved between her legs. Just when she thought his skilled fingers were going to give her another orgasm, they stopped. Before she could utter a complaint, his hot mouth took their place.

Delaney learned that not all orgasms were alike. The last one had been like a shower of electric sparks. This one detonated in an explosion of intense sensations that had her moaning so loudly she had to muffle the sound with a pillow as his tongue drew out her climax until she was nothing but a mass of quivering nerves.

When her body had given its last shiver of satisfaction, Shane's mouth left her and he kissed his way up to her mouth. He kissed her deeply and thoroughly before he drew back.

"You okay?"

All she could do was hum. "Mmm-hmm."

Through the dark, she saw his flash of white teeth. He settled at her side and pulled her close.

She waited for the next part.

The actual sex part.

But all he did was slid his fingers up and down her back in a soft caress. Maybe he was waiting for her to do something. He had certainly done his part. Now it was her turn to do hers.

She reached between them and touched him. She was surprised how hard he was . . . and how soft and smooth his skin was as she caressed the thick length. She knew he liked it by the way his body tensed, but she also knew she wasn't doing it right. She wanted to give him the same pleasure he'd given her. She wanted it badly.

"Show me," she said. "Show me how to make you feel like you made me feel."

He covered her hand with his and guided her in a strong up-and-down stroke that had his breath quickening. The sound of his pleasure made her feel powerful and sexy. She took over and watched as his lips parted and his eyes rolled back before they closed. She felt like she'd just gotten the hang of it when he stopped her and pushed her to her back.

His eyes were intent. "Are you sure, Del? Are you sure this is what you want?"

"It's what I want." She brushed back a strand of his hair that had fallen over his forehead. "You're what I want."

He kissed her before he drew away and grabbed his jeans from the floor. Once he had the condom on, he shifted over her. "If at any time, you want me to—"

She pressed a finger to his lips. "Be quiet, honey buns, and just do it."

It did hurt. But just until she adjusted to the feel. Then it felt like a stretching of tight muscles. When he started to move, the feeling turned to more of a pleasurable ache. With each stroke, the ache grew.

She needed more friction and started to move. Awkwardly at first, but then she was synchronizing her hip thrusts with his in a perfect rhythm that felt like riding. When her orgasm hit, Shane's hit too.

They rode it out together with their gazes locked and their breaths held.

When it was over, Delaney was no longer a virgin.

She was also head over heels in love.

Chapter Sixteen

"What do you mean you're not giving my boot back?" Delaney tugged at the hair on Shane's chest. "Those are my favorite boots. I have them worn in just right."

Shane covered her hand with his and kissed the top of her head. "Sorry, princess. You left it, you lost it."

She lifted her head from his chest and glared at him. He couldn't help grinning. He loved her feistiness. "I didn't leave it. You drove off with it."

"Because I had a gun pointed at me." Shane glanced at the bedroom door. "I'm surprised Uncle Jack hasn't shown up this morning. I'm sure your family has discovered you're not in your bedroom by now. You probably should've gone back early this morning."

"Thus says the man who told me I needed to grow up."

He cringed. "I was feeling a little angry last night and said some things I shouldn't have said."

She propped her chin on her folded hands and stared back at him with lake-blue eyes a man could easily drown in. "Jealous?"

"Horribly."

She grinned. "Then we're even. I was jealous as hell. Not just of Everly, but also of Mystic. I couldn't stand the thought of her getting to run her fingers through your hair when I couldn't."

"Ahh, that's why she cancelled my appointment."

"Buck was responsible for that."

"Is there something going on between the two of them?"

"They both say no, but sometimes it's hard to admit your feelings for a friend." She hesitated. "Were you in love with Everly?"

He shook his head. "I was only with her once and it was a tequila mistake. I've never thought of Everly as anything but a friend."

Her crystal-blue gaze grew intense. "And what about me? Am I just a friend?"

Shane still hadn't untangled the intense feelings he had for Delaney. But he knew one thing. She wasn't just a friend.

"You're more than a friend, Delaney." He smiled and tried to lighten the mood. "And you can run your hands through my hair whenever you want, cowgirl."

A wicked twinkle entered her eyes and she slid a hand under the covers. "Even here?" He groaned as her fingers slid through his pubic hair and wrapped around his cock.

He closed his eyes as she stroked him to life. "Del . . . we should probably get dressed and go down to breakfast so your family doesn't think I'm holding you hostage."

"Not likely. No man could hold me hostage . . . unless I wanted him to." She sent him a seductive smile and ducked her head under the covers. What she did with her mouth had him going from semi-erect to steel in seconds. It didn't take much for him to be hanging from the climax ledge. He didn't want to fall alone. He drew her up until she was straddling him. For just a second, he slid inside her and felt the nirvana of slick, hot skin on slick, hot skin.

But he couldn't stay.

"I need to get a condom." He went to lift her off him, but she adjusted her hips and took him deeper. They both moaned at the heavenly sensation.

She flexed, and his eyes rolled back. "Why? I'm on birth control and you told me last night that you were just recently checked. So why do you need a condom?" He tried to come up with a good reason, but damned if he could when he was in the grip of Delaney's wet heat. Then she started to move and he completely lost his train of thought.

She rode him hard and steady, her thigh muscles flexing as she lifted and then sank deep. She rode him until, just like the horses she trained, he was willing to do whatever she asked. She only seemed to want one thing—to drive him wild. She did. Every roll of her hips had him groaning and begging for more. When he couldn't take the slow pace a second longer, he rolled her over and thrust into her as her legs cradled his hips. He didn't last long. He tumbled over the ledge and he felt her orgasm tighten around him. There was no way to describe the intensity of the climax that rocked him.

A few minutes later, he came back to reality with Delaney draped over his chest. For the first time in a long time, his mind wasn't filled with the stress of what he needed to get done. There was no urgency to get the app finished. No strong need to prove himself and make his first million. In fact, he didn't care anything about getting back to his computer. He just wanted to stay right where he was . . . in the arms of this cowgirl.

So he did.

They stayed in the room for the rest of the morning. They took a shower. Which resulted in some soapy, sexy fun. Then they climbed back in bed and made love again. Around noon, a knock sounded on the door. Shane figured their time was up and if he didn't answer it, Delaney's brothers would bust it down. Leaving her snoozing, he got up and got dressed before he opened the door.

But instead of Stetson, Wolfe, or Buck standing there, it was Adeline holding a tray of food in front of her rounded stomach.

"I figured y'all might be hungry."

He took the tray from her. "Thank you." He awkwardly stood there searching for something to say. "Delaney is fine."

Adeline smiled. "I know. Delaney is never going to do something she doesn't want to do."

He should have just kept his mouth shut. But

he couldn't. "I don't know about that. I think she does a lot of things she doesn't want to do to please her family."

Adeline's smile faded, but she didn't disagree. "Then maybe you can help her find her voice like Gage helped me." She turned and headed down the hallway. "Enjoy the rest of your day."

When she was gone, Shane bumped the door closed with his shoulder and carried the tray over to the bed where Delaney was now sitting up. By the intense look on her face, he knew she'd heard the conversation he'd had with her sister.

"I'm sorry," he said as he placed the tray on the bed. "I had no business saying that."

She plumped a pillow behind her back. "Why? It's true. I have done things to please my family and not myself."

He joined her on the bed and handed her one of the cups of coffee. "So what would please you, Delaney Kingman?"

"You please me."

The happy feeling in his stomach made him grin like a fool. "You please me too. But what else?"

She thought for a moment before she spoke. "I want to work with abused and abandoned animals. And not just when I can make time. I want to start a refuge."

He picked up a fork and cut into the stack of blueberry pancakes and then offered her the bite. "Then do it."

"Maybe I will." She took the bite and smiled.

They didn't talk much after that. Instead, they

fed each other pancakes, cheesy scrambled eggs, and fried potatoes with onions and red bell peppers. When they'd almost cleared the tray of food, Shane reclined back on the pillows and groaned.

"I think I'm in love with your sister."

She held out the last bite of pancakes. "She only delivered it. It was Potts who made it."

He took the bite. "Then I'm in love with Potts."

"Ahh, so you're one of those men whose heart is connected to his stomach. Then you'll never fall for me, honey buns, I can't cook a lick."

He moved the tray from between them and pressed her back to the pillows. "I'd rather have a cowgirl who can ride than a woman who can cook any day."

The next few weeks passed by in a blur of contentment for Shane. Delaney moved into his room and the Kingmans didn't say a word about it. Although it was obvious by Stetson's and Wolfe's dark scowls whenever Shane ran into them that they weren't too pleased by the arrangement.

But the rest of the Kingmans seemed to be fine with it. Buck invited him to a poker game in the bunkhouse—as long as he didn't bring Delaney. (Which Shane did and she ended up winning everyone's money.) Gretchen made him his favorite coconut cream pie and started ironing his shirts in return for his help updating Nasty Jack's social media pages. Lily asked him about doing an interactive app for her Fairy Prairie series. And Adeline asked for his help with the ranch website.

Shane didn't have a problem helping the Kingmans. He had the time. He couldn't do much more on his senior citizen app without hiring more experienced developers. Since he hadn't heard back from Dan Fuller, he didn't have the money. He probably should contact other investors. But he was no longer in any hurry to start his business. Maybe he would continue to freelance for a while. Or maybe he'd just take some time off and hang out on the ranch. He'd discovered that he not only liked goats, he liked dogs and cats and even horses.

Which was how he found himself searching out Buck in the stables one afternoon when Delaney had gone to check out an abused mule at the animal humane society.

"You want me to teach you how to ride a horse?" Buck said. "Why don't you ask Delaney? Don't tell her I said so, but she's the best rider on the ranch."

"I want to surprise her."

Buck studied him for a long moment before he nodded. "Okay, then. Let's start with the basics."

There turned out to be a lot of basics to riding a horse. Before Shane could start riding, he had to learn how to saddle the mare Buck chose for him. Once he mastered saddling, Buck showed him how to mount and dismount and adjust the stirrups and hold the reins.

Finally, Buck led the horse out into the paddock where he sat on the railing and issued orders to Shane or yelled at him for doing something wrong. Shane had to learn how to guide the mare in a circle, then get her to go from a walk to a trot to a gallop. The trot bounced him worse than Delaney's four-wheeling. The gallop had him hanging on for dear life.

But he refused to give up.

"So how did I do?" he asked when Buck had him guide the horse back into the stables.

"For a greenhorn, okay. But you'll need a lot more practice if you want to keep up with Delaney."

Shane dismounted. "Then I'll practice."

Buck studied him as he took the reins. "I guess I was wrong."

"About what?"

"I thought your engagement was too quick and you were more in lust than love. But it looks like you *are* in love with my sister."

Shane couldn't have felt more surprised if Buck had punched him in the face. He stood there feeling completely off-kilter as Tab came out of a stall and started talking to Buck about a sick mare. Needing some air, Shane walked out of the stables and tried to collect his thoughts.

Love? The word scared the hell out of him. Love came with a lot of baggage and commitment. He was only twenty-seven years old. He wasn't ready for love. There was so much he wanted to do first. Like start his company and make his first million. Love had never been part of the equation. Sure, he'd thought about getting married and having kids. But later in life. Much later. Not now.

The ring of his cellphone startled him out of

his thoughts. Thankful for the distraction, he quickly answered it.

"Shane Ransom."

"Hi, Shane, this is Dan Fuller. I've got some good news. After doing some research, I've decided to invest in your app. I think you have a winner."

It took a minute for Shane to react. "Uhh . . . that's great."

"Now all we need to do is iron out the details. Can you and your lawyer meet me and mine on Thursday to finalize everything?"

"This Thursday?" That was only two days away.

"Unless that doesn't work for you."

Shane shook his head to clear it. "No. That's fine."

"Great," Dan said. "Afterwards, I'll take you to see the vacant office building I own in Fort Worth. I think it would work perfectly for your needs."

Shane didn't know why he hesitated. He'd always planned on being based in Dallas and now he'd been offered a place to start his company. A place where he could hire a lot more developers and make a lot more money. He'd be a fool not to jump at the chance. "Sounds good, sir. See you soon."

After he hung up, he should have felt elated. Instead, he felt . . . disconnected. Like he'd stepped into someone else's dream and not his own.

But this *was* his dream. It had always been his dream. And he needed to pull his head out and remember that. He might like Delaney. He might even love her. But this wasn't the time for love. He had money to make. His goal to achieve. He was a software developer who lived in Dallas. He wasn't a goat babysitter with a beautiful cowgirl fiancée who lived on a ranch.

"Hey, honey buns."

He glanced up from the phone he still held in his hand to see his beautiful cowgirl fiancée striding toward him. Her hair was in braids and she wore a battered straw cowboy hat that had been munched on by Karl the Goat and her shirt had mud on it—and possibly something else. And yet, she looked more beautiful than any woman he had ever seen in his life. The emotion that swelled up inside him was difficult to ignore.

But he did.

He pinned on a smile. "Hey! I was just going to call you." He lamely held up the phone. "I got an investor."

Her smile got even bigger, and she rushed over and flung her arms around his neck. "That's awesome, Shane."

"Yeah." He squeezed his eyes shut and breathed in her earthy scent before he drew back. "I need to head to Dallas." He swallowed the lump that had moved to the back of his throat. "Today."

"Today?"

"Yeah. I need to meet with my lawyers before I meet with Dan on Thursday."

The sparkle in her eyes faded, along with her smile. She stepped back. "Oh . . . umm . . . so when are you coming back?"

"That's the thing." He swallowed hard, but it

didn't help. The lump was growing bigger by the second. "I'll have a lot to do with hiring developers and getting the app launched. So I probably won't have a lot of time."

She stared at him. "So you're not coming back."

The lump had grown too big to let words pass. All he could do was shake his head.

He read the hurt in her eyes. It was like a sharp dagger straight through his heart. But, thankfully, Delaney wasn't one to stay hurt for long. Her chin came up and when she spoke there wasn't one quiver in her voice.

"Then that's that. You don't have to say anything to my family. I'll tell them." She went to walk past him, but he couldn't let her go. His hand shot out and stopped her.

"Delaney." His voice shook. "I'm sorry."

Her blue eyes looked directly back at him. "For what? We both knew it was fake."

"But it wasn't fake."

She smiled sadly. "It wasn't real either." She pulled from him and walked away.

Chapter Seventeen

D ELANEY DID WHAT she always did when her emotions were in turmoil. She worked her butt off so she didn't have to think. She spent the rest of the day helping with spring branding. It was hot and dirty work and she was exhausted by the time she got back to the ranch. While she was feeding the goats, she got a tiny ache in her chest and a burning behind her eyes. But that probably had more to do with it being time to wean the baby goats. She would miss feeding the kids.

After she finished with the goats, she headed to the stables and helped Tab muck out stalls. She was spraying off the main floor of the stables when the water suddenly shut off and the hose deflated.

She turned to see Adeline standing by the spigot with a concerned look on her face. This was one of the reasons Delaney hadn't wanted to go back to the house. She hadn't wanted to deal with her family's reaction to Shane leaving. But it looked like they weren't going to give her a choice.

She forced her brightest smile. "Hey, Addie."

She glanced out the opposite door at the setting sun. "I didn't realize it was so late. I guess Potts already has dinner on the table. I just need to finish up here and I'll be right up." She glanced down at her filthy clothes. "Although I probably better take a shower first. Potts hates dirt more than he hates tardiness."

Adeline stepped closer. Even over seven months pregnant, her sister moved with grace. "What happened, Del? Why did Shane go back to Dallas?"

So Shane *had* left. Deep down, Delaney had held on to a spark of hope that he'd have a change of heart and when she went back to the castle, she'd find him sitting at the table with the rest of her family. It was a foolish hope.

She started rolling up the hose. "He got the financing to launch his new app and start a software development company."

"Is he coming back?"

A wall of tears swelled, but she blinked them away. "No. I just felt like it was best to break off the engagement. I mean there's no way I can move to Dallas. And he can't start his business from here."

Adeline turned Delaney around and pulled her close to her rounded belly. "I'm so sorry, Del."

Delaney melted into her sister's embrace. But she only enjoyed the balm of Adeline's love for a few seconds before she stepped away. "Now don't go gettin' all weepy, Addie. I'm fine. I was the one who broke it off with Shane."

"But why? I know I was against your engagement at first, but then I saw how happy Shane made you and I realized my mistake. I had no business talking about rushing your engagement when I rushed into marriage with Gage. And Stetson had no business talking about you two not having anything in common when Lily spends all day on her computer and he spends all day working the ranch. She couldn't ride a horse either until just a few months ago. But that didn't stop Stetson from falling for her. I'm sure you and Shane can work out your differences. And your living arrangements."

"It wasn't just about our differences or our living arrangements." She told the truth. "The engagement was fake, Addie. We only lied so Chance wouldn't lose his job. So there's no reason to be worried about me. Your baby sister is going to be just fine. Just like I always am."

Adeline stared at her. "It was all a hoax? But I don't understand. You seemed so happy the last few weeks."

She *had* been happy. Happier than she'd ever been in her life. And now she just felt . . . sad and empty. But she wasn't about to tell her sister that. "It's called good sex," she said with a forced smile. "Good sex can make a person happy."

"And what about Shane? Was it just sex for him too?"

She turned away and started rerolling the hose just to give her shaking hands something to do. "Why else would he leave? Now I better get this hose rolled up tight or Tab will give me hell. Tell Potts I'll be in in a minute."

She could feel her sister's hesitation, but, thankfully, Adeline gave in and left the stables. When she was gone, Delaney released her breath and rested her head against the stable wall.

"I guess it's not easy being the tough kid who doesn't cause her family any worry."

Delaney turned to see Uncle Jack standing in the hallway that led to Tab's room.

She straightened and forced another smile. "Hey, Uncle Jack. What are you up to?"

"I come down here in the evenings to play chess with Tab. Potts can play dominos, but he sucks at chess." He shuffled over to the bench by the door and sat down, his breathing heavy. It had only been a few months since his heart attack so Delaney was instantly concerned.

"You okay, Uncle Jack?"

"I'm fine. Walking around this ranch is much harder than walking around my bar. But Doc Walt says exercise is good for me." He snorted. "As if my old ticker can be fixed. Despite what the doc says, I believe your heart only has so many beats before it quits for good. Exercise will only hasten my death."

He glanced up at her. "I also believe that your heart knows when it finds a perfect match. A heart doesn't care if a person can ride a horse or knows how to work one of those damn computers. It just knows what it feels. And I think your heart feels more than you're lettin' on."

"I'm fine, Uncle Jack."

"Of course you are. Just like I was fine after my Mary died. After my son died. After my grandson died. I was just fine and dandy. I wanted everyone to know I was a tough old bird who could handle anything." He paused and she was shocked to see tears glisten in his eyes. "Then Wolfe and Gretchen showed up. They made me realize being tough and pretending like you don't feel anything is just plain stupid." He tapped his chest. "And bad for the heart. You can look this stubborn old cowboy in the eyes and tell me that you didn't feel anything for Shane, but I won't believe you like Adeline did. You felt more than lust for that boy and I know it."

Delaney didn't know what happened. One second, she was standing there being strong and the next second she was bawling like a newborn calf who couldn't find its mama. She cried even harder when Uncle Jack stood and pulled her against his frail chest.

"That's it, girlie. Let it all out."

She did. She cried until she felt like a wrung-out dishtowel. Uncle Jack just held her and patted her back. She might have continued to sob if Buck hadn't walked into the stables.

"What's the holdup, Del? Stetson is getting pissed that you haven't—hey, Uncle Jack. Stetson's been looking for you too. It's dinnertime and . . . what's going on? Are you cryin', Del?"

She started to make up some excuse about having something in her eye, but then stopped. Uncle Jack was right. Sometimes you just needed to get your feelings out.

"Yes, I'm cryin'," she said. "Sometimes people cry. And I don't need your permission."

Buck held up his hands and took a step back. "I didn't say you did. I was just wondering if you're okay."

She glanced at Uncle Jack, and he lifted a bushy eyebrow. She looked back at Buck. "No. I'm not okay. I fell in love with Shane and I'm upset that's he's gone."

"But Adeline just said you were fine."

"I lied to Addie. I've been lying a lot lately. Mostly to myself." Tears started dripping down her cheeks again. Buck freaked out.

"Okay . . . umm, well . . . do you want me to go get Shane and bring him back? I figure me and Wolfe can get him hogtied and in the bed of my truck without any problems."

"No!" Delaney said. "The last thing I need is my brothers getting involved in this. I'm an adult woman. It's my problem. Not yours."

"So what are you going to do?"

"There's nothing to do. If Shane loved me, he would've stayed."

"That's not necessarily true," Uncle Jack said. "Men can be real idiots at times. The only way to find out if Shane loves you is to ask him."

"What if he doesn't?"

Uncle Jack patted her shoulder. "Then you'll cry some more and get over it. But at least you'll know where you stand."

"What the hell is going on?" Stetson walked into the stables. "First, Adeline comes back without you. Then I send Buck and he disappears too. And what are you doing here, Uncle Jack? You should be up at the house for dinner."

Uncle Jack scowled. "I appreciate you giving me a home, boy. But there's something you need to learn. You ain't my keeper. If I want to skip dinner, I'll skip dinner."

Stetson's scowl matched Uncle Jack's. "This family eats together."

"In my opinion, this family does way too much together. And you have gotten a little too used to callin' all the shots with your siblings. I get it. You helped raise them and it's hard to let go." He paused. "I had the same problem. I ran my son off with my orders. And we all know what happened to my grandson. I don't want the same thing happening to you, Stetson. Your siblings are adults. You can ask your family to eat together. But you can't order them to. There are times when a person needs to break free of the chain of command and make their own decisions. Now, if you'll excuse me, I think I'll head up for dinner. I'm starving. Come on, Buck."

Buck hesitated and looked at Stetson. "I think I'll pass on dinner tonight. I'm going to head into town and see if Mystic wants to go to Nasty Jack's."

Uncle Jack snorted. "When are you going to marry that girl?"

"Marry Mystic?" Buck laughed as they disappeared into the twilight night.

When they were gone, Stetson looked at Delaney and sighed. "I never should've invited Uncle Jack to come live with us."

"Worried we're all going to jump ship on you, Stet?" she teased.

His eyes turned sad. "I wouldn't blame you if you did. Uncle Jack is right. I really screwed up the entire parenting thing, didn't I? How the hell am I going to father my own child?"

She walked over and placed an arm around his shoulders. Shoulders that seemed broad, but not broad enough for the weight he'd had to carry. "You're going to be an amazing father, Stet. You were the best parent I could've asked for. Unlike Daddy, you always had time for me—you taught me how to be the cowgirl I am. Yeah, you might be stubborn and gruff, but I've never doubted for a second that you love me and want what's best for me." She hesitated. "It's just that you can't figure out what's best for people. They have to figure that out on their own."

He studied her. "And have you figured it out?"

She nodded. "I've figured out what I want. I've also figured out that you can't always get what you want." Tears dripped from her eyes and Stetson pulled her into his arms for a tight hug.

"I guess this is about Shane."

She nodded against his chest.

"So your engagement wasn't the hoax you told Adeline it was. At least on your side." He hesitated. "I didn't plan on telling you this, Del, but I got a call from a man named Dan Fuller the other day. He's the investor Shane has been talking to. He called to make sure you and Shane were really engaged. I guess Shane dropped the Kingman name during their meeting. I'm thinking saving Chance's job wasn't the only reason Shane wanted to pretend to be engaged."

The news should've made her angry. And it did. Just not at Shane.

She drew back. "And you haven't dropped people's names before to get ahead in business? Shane is just as driven as you are, Stet. Which is probably one of the reasons I fell for him. He knows what he wants and goes after it. That doesn't make him a bad person. If he used our name to get the backing he needed, then more power to him. He never once asked me, or anyone in the family, for money. And he could have. I won't have you thinking badly of him just because—"

"Whoa." Stetson held up his hands. "Okay, Del. I was just trying to make you feel better about Shane leaving."

"Nothing is going to make me feel better about Shane leaving, Stet. But I can't blame him for following his dream. Just like he can't blame me for needing to stay on the ranch."

There was a long stretch of silence before Stetson spoke. "Needing to stay or wanting to stay?"

She shrugged. "The ranch is as much my responsibility as it is yours. I can't just walk away from it."

"You sound like me, Del. But sometimes we need to walk away from our responsibilities. Especially when they keep us from getting what we really want."

"You would never walk away from your responsibilities."

"I thought the same thing until I met Lily. Then I was willing to leave everything and head to England to be with her."

Delaney stared at him. "You were planning on living in England?"

He nodded. "If that's what it had taken to keep her. Sometimes you have to make tough choices for your own happiness. What's going to make you happy, Del?"

The answer wasn't long in coming. "Shane."

"Then I guess you need to go after him."

"But what if he doesn't want me coming after him?"

"From what I saw, I doubt that's the case." Stetson smiled and ruffled her hair. "And when my little sister sets her mind on something, she usually doesn't give up until she gets what she wants." He winked. "It's the Kingman way."

Chapter Eighteen

"WHAT ARE YOU doing?"

Shane glanced up from the empty shot glass he'd been staring into. Wolfe stood on the other side of the bar. He wasn't scowling. He looked confused—with good reason. What was Shane doing at Nasty Jack's bar drowning his sorrows when he should be in Dallas celebrating his good fortune?

"I needed a drink," he said. It was the truth. As soon as he stepped into his small, dreary Dallas apartment, he *had* needed a drink. He just shouldn't have driven all the way back to Cursed to get it.

"I can see that," Wolfe said. "You've downed five shots in less than ten minutes. Did you and Delaney get in a fight?"

He should have simply nodded and left it at that. Instead, the tequila had him rambling. "It wasn't a fight. I wish it had been. If she had yelled and cussed and screamed at me, at least I would've known that she cared. But she just walked away and didn't look back. Not once." He shook his head. "And it's for the best. She loves her family and the ranch and I can't see her living anywhere else. Even though she probably should."

Wolfe's eyes narrowed. "What are you talking about? Delaney belongs on the ranch."

Shane nodded. "You're right. But she also needs some breathing room from her overprotective family who thinks she's still a kid." Regardless of Wolfe's deepening scowl, he couldn't seem to shut up. "Delaney has great ideas for improving the ranch, but y'all refuse to listen to her. She's not a kid. She's a grown woman. An intelligent ... funny ... beautiful ... extremely hot woman."

An image of just how hot she was all naked and tangled in sheets popped into his head. The fantasy dissolved when Wolfe smacked him in the face with the towel he'd been using to wipe off the bar.

"Are you fantasizing about my sister while I'm standing right here, asshole?"

Shane blinked. "N-o-o-o."

Wolfe rolled his eyes and shook his head before he lowered the towel. "Okay, you might have a point. Stetson gave me the job of watching out for Delaney and Buck and maybe I took it too seriously. Maybe we all did. It's hard to think of your little siblings as grown adults. You're right. We need to give Delaney more credit. She's worked hard to make the ranch what it is today."

"Damn right, she has. Have you seen how good she is with animals? She's Delaney Dolittle. There's not an animal she can't tame. And goats. Goats follow her around like she's their mama." A wave of sadness washed over him. "Damn, I'm going to miss those kids." He looked at Wolfe who was watching him intently. "Have you seen them? They're cute as hell." He chuckled. "And that Dopey is quite the character."

He pulled out his cellphone and tapped on his photos. He turned the phone to Wolfe and scrolled through the pictures of the baby goats he'd taken. The goats and Delaney. In every picture, she was right in the middle of the kids—feeding them bottles, cuddling them close, or smiling at Shane.

Wolfe studied the picture before he looked at Shane. "You must love her if you can put up with her goats."

There was that word again. The word he was trying so hard to ignore.

"If you're going to be with Delaney," Wolfe continued. "You need to know that she's got a temper and is impulsive. She usually acts before she thinks." The phone rang and he headed down the bar to answer it, calling over his shoulder. "Just give her time, Shane. She'll get over whatever ticked her off."

Shane shook his head and mumbled to himself. "No, she won't. Not this time." He was the one who had acted impulsive. The one who had made a stupid decision without thinking it through. Delaney would never forgive him. He wasn't sure he could forgive himself.

He was sitting there wishing he'd asked Wolfe for another shot of tequila—or the entire bottle—when Everly came strutting into the bar in tight skinny jeans and a leather vest that showed off her tat.

"Things must be bad if you're drinking tequila." She slipped onto the barstool next to Shane. "I thought you swore it off after our wild night together. Or was there something else in that empty shot glass? Milk, perhaps?"

"What are you doing here, Ev?"

"Your brother called me and said you could use a friend." She held out her hands. "So here I am!"

Shane mentally cussed himself out for calling Chance on his way back to Cursed and spilling his guts—then inviting him for a drink at Nasty Jack's. As if his brother would drop his Bible and head to a bar. But Chance shouldn't have called Everly to keep an eye on him.

"You didn't need to drive all the way from Dallas," he said. "I'm fine."

"Sure you are. That's why you're sitting there with that pathetic hangdog look." Everly glanced down the bar. "What does it take to get a drink around here?" She waved a hand to get Wolfe's attention, but he was too engrossed in his phone conversation to notice. She sighed. "It's so hard to get good help these days." She hefted herself up on the bar and jumped behind it. After grabbing a bottle of tequila and another shot glass, she headed back to Shane. The cowboy sitting two stools away stopped her.

"Hey, sweetheart, could you get me a Coors Light?"

She set the tequila and shot glass in front of Shane before she flipped open the cooler and checked out the labels on the bottles tucked into ice. When she found the right one, she grabbed the turnkey hanging from the side of the cooler and opened the bottle. Before she could even finish placing the beer on a cocktail napkin, the woman next to the cowboy asked for a gin and tonic. Everly rolled her eyes at Shane, but she fixed it for the woman before she walked back over to Shane and poured them each a shot.

"So what shall we drink to this time? Your first million?" She hesitated. "Or maybe pretty cowgirls?"

Definitely not pretty cowgirls. He lifted his glass. "To making my first million." He downed his shot, but Everly didn't drink hers. "Something wrong?" he asked.

She crinkled her nose. "Yeah. That toast just didn't sound sincere."

"Excuse me?"

She set down her shot glass. "Or maybe it wasn't the toast as much as your eyes when you said it. Every other time you've made that toast, your eyes have held this greedy gleam. This time there was no gleam at all. Which leads me to believe that you aren't as hungry for money as you used to be." She tipped her head. "You wouldn't be hungry for something else, would you, Shane Ransom? Like maybe the love of that pretty cowgirl you refused to toast?"

"Leave it alone, Ev."

"Sorry, but that's not what good friends do. Good friends don't let a wound fester. They pop it, squeeze it, and get all the nasty pus out."

Shane cringed at the visual. "Thanks, but I don't have a festering wound."

She rapped him in the head with her knuckles. "No. You just have a hard head. Which is why you're sitting here in this dive bar trying to drown your sorrows in tequila." She downed the shot and slammed the glass on the bar. "So let me spell it out for you. You're in love with the cowgirl—I know, it doesn't make any sense why you couldn't fall in love with someone more like you. A big city girl who would love to spend all that money you planned on making on stiletto boots and tattoos." She shrugged. "But, apparently, love doesn't work like that. Apparently, hearts don't listen to common sense. They just go rogue and do exactly what they want to do. And we pitiful humans are stuck dealing with the illogical muscle thumping beneath our rib cages." She grabbed his cheeks between her hands. "Is any of this making sense to you, Shaney? Or am I going to have to repeat this entire spiel in the morning after you sober up?"

He wished he was too drunk for Everly's words to make sense. But he wasn't. The muscle beneath his rib cage *had* gone rogue and now he was paying for it. "I love her, Ev."

Everly released his face and patted him on the head. "Good boy. That wasn't so hard, was it?"

"But it doesn't matter what I feel. Delaney would never leave the ranch. And I just got financing for my new app. It's what I've dreamed about all my life."

"Then I guess you have a choice to make. What dream do you want the most? Although, if you came all the way back to Cursed, I'd say you already made your decision. You just needed some liquid courage before you headed to the ranch to beg for Delaney's forgiveness."

Everly was too damn smart for her own good.

"So when I get there, what do I say?" he asked.

"How about, 'This started out as a fake engagement, but I'm not faking now. I love you and want to spend the rest of my life showing you just how much. You are my stars and my moon and my sun. When you walk into a room, I get an immediate boner and want to take you right there—'"

Shane held up a hand. "Okay, I get the picture."

"Do you?"

"Yeah, I get what you think I should do. But you're thinking that Delaney's feelings are as strong as mine. She cares about me, but I don't think she loves me. If she did, she would have told me. She's one of the most honest women I've ever met—besides you. She wouldn't have kept that a secret from me."

A sad smile spread over Everly's face. "You'd be surprised how good honest women are at hiding their true feelings. Now get your butt up and go get your—"

Before she could finish, Wolfe stepped up behind her. The scowl was back. This time twice as fierce. "What the hell did you do?"

Everly turned to him. "Now don't get your panties in a bunch, hot bartender guy. I'm sorry I encroached on your territory, but my friend here really needed a drink and you were busy so I figured you wouldn't mind if we helped ourselves—oh, and that cowboy and his girlfriend. They owe you money for a beer and a gin and tonic. But the tip is mine."

Wolfe blinked at her. "I wasn't talking to you." His gaze zeroed in on Shane. "I was talking to him. What the hell did you do to Delaney?" He reached across the bar and grabbed Shane by the front of his shirt, lifting him off the barstool. "You have two seconds to answer before I bust your face."

"Oh, goody." Everly clapped her hands. "A country bar fight. But can you wait to kick Shane's ass until I get my phone. My followers are going to want pictures of this."

As Wolfe stared at her in confusion, Chance walked through the door. His brother must've been worried about him to show up at a bar.

"Why if it isn't saintly Chance?" Everly said. "I guess you didn't trust me to handle things."

"Considering I walked in to find Shane in Wolfe's clutches, I'd say I had reason not to trust you to handle the situation." Chance turned to Wolfe. "Let go of my brother."

Wolfe arched an eyebrow. "And if I don't?"

"This night just keeps getting better," Everly said. "Not only am I going to get to see my first bar brawl. But I'm also going to get to see Mister Goody-Two-Shoes get his saintly ass kicked." She held her arms over her head. "Score! But first I need to get my phone." She hopped back up on the bar. "Excuse me, Wolfe, but could you let go of Shane and move for just a second while I swing my legs over?" Wolfe released Shane and stepped out of the way. "Thank you." Everly swung her legs over the bar, then looked at Shane and mouthed "Run."

It was too bad the tequila had slowed Shane's reaction time. He no more than got up from the barstool, than Wolfe jumped over the bar. But before Wolfe could grab Shane, Chance did something very un-preacher like and punched him, knocking Wolfe back against the bar. Before Shane could tell his brother that it was his fight, Buck came charging out of nowhere and hit Chance. Then Shane had to hit Buck. Which resulted in Wolfe throwing a punch at Shane that sent him reeling.

After that, everything became a blur of throwing punches and receiving them . . . until a gunshot rang out.

Shane lowered his fist and weaved on his feet, squinting through his swelling eyes for the person who had fired the shot. He was surprised to see Gretchen standing there, pointing a gun at the ceiling.

"I think that will be just about enough."

Wolfe stared at his wife in shock. "Where the hell did you get that gun, Red?"

"It's Uncle Jack's. He showed me where it was just in case I needed to stop a bar brawl. I didn't realize my own husband would be right in the middle of it."

"In the middle of it," Everly said. "He started it."

Gretchen's eyes narrowed and Wolfe held up his hands. "Now, honey, I had just cause. Shane hurt Delaney and made her cry. And you know Del never cries."

Shane turned to him. "Delaney cried?"

"I witnessed it myself," Buck said. "She was sobbing her heart out over you."

Before he could absorb the information, the door flew open and a sheriff and deputy charged in. But Shane was too stunned to pay any attention as the sheriff started asking questions. Or even when he handcuffed Shane, Wolfe, Chance, and Buck and tossed them into the back of a patrol car.

All the way to jail, all Shane could think about was one thing.

Delaney had cried.

His tough cowgirl had cried.

Chapter Nineteen

After making the decision to talk to Shane, Delaney had wanted to leave for Dallas right then. But Stetson talked her into waiting until she'd had a good night's sleep. Seeing as how she'd worked herself to death in an attempt to not have to deal with her feelings, it was a good idea. She was mentally and physically exhausted and fell asleep as soon as her head hit the pillow.

She woke the next morning feeling refreshed . . . and terrified. As convinced as Stetson was that Kingmans always got what they wanted, Delaney wasn't so sure. If Shane didn't love her, she couldn't make him. What she could do was make a fool of herself.

By the time she got down to breakfast, she was more than second-guessing her decision to talk with Shane. She was hoping for a little pep talk from her family. But she stopped short when she saw Buck's and Wolfe's battered faces.

"What the hell happened to you two?"

"Watch your mouth at my table," Potts scolded as he set a pitcher of orange juice down.

"Sorry, Potts, but I'm a little shocked to see my

brothers looking like they've been in a bar fight."

Uncle Jack snorted. "Because they were in a bar fight."

Delaney took a seat at the table. "With who?"

Uncle Jack started to answer when Wolfe cut in. "Now I don't think we need to bore Del with the details."

"You're only saying that because you know what she's going to do when she finds out who it is," Uncle Jack said.

"And she has every right to be angry," Gretchen huffed. "I'm still so mad I could spit, Wolfe Kingman."

Wolfe smiled and then winced. Delaney figured his swollen lip hurt like hell. "Now, Red, I thought we made up last night after you bailed me out of jail."

"Jail?" Delaney said. "You were in jail?"

"*We* were in jail." Buck held a bag of frozen blueberries to his eye. By the grin on his face, he wasn't too upset about spending the night in jail, or his black eyes.

Stetson didn't find it as amusing. "That's nothing to brag about, Buck."

"Now don't get all holier than thou," Uncle Jack said. "Spending one night in jail is good for a man. Teaches them valuable lessons."

"Obviously, it hasn't taught Wolfe anything." Gretchen glared at her husband. "And if you think I'm going to put up with our child's daddy starting brawls, you've got another think coming. My mama always says, 'A smart man speaks with his mouth, not his fists.'"

"You're right, Red. I shouldn't have let my temper—"Wolfe's eyes widened. "Our child?"

Gretchen's eyes softened. "I was going to tell you last night after we closed the bar, but instead I was bailing you out of jail. This morning, you are going to come with me to church. You need to do a little repent—"

Wolfe kissed her and cut her off. When he drew back his bruised face was glowing. "I'll repent all you want, Red. I give you my word. No more fights. I just got upset when I heard that Delaney cried. Still, I wouldn't have hit Shane if his brother hadn't gotten into it." He cringed as soon as the words were out of his mouth and he glanced at Delaney. "Now, Del, before you go off the deep end. I pulled my punches."

Delaney stared at her brother. "You punched Shane?" She looked at Buck. "You both ganged up on Shane?"

Buck held up his hands. "We didn't gang up on Shane. He and the preacher gave as good as they got." He winked at Wolfe. "Although I'd say we won." He moved his jaw back and forth. "But the preacher does have a good right hook. I'll give him that."

"Urrgh!" Delaney growled. "What happened? And I mean I want to hear every detail."

Wolfe and Buck took turns telling the story. When they were finished, Delaney was no longer concerned about Shane getting beat up by her brothers. She wanted to beat him up too.

"He was drinking tequila shots at the bar with Everly?" While she was bawling her eyes out? She had never been so angry in her life. He had said he had to get back to Dallas, but it seemed he had plenty of time to party with Everly at Nasty Jack's.

Delaney had thought their relationship meant something to him. At least, enough to be upset it was over. Instead, he'd been celebrating the end of his engagement with shots of tequila . . . in her hometown bar! No, she wasn't just mad. She was furious. And the man wasn't going to get to leave town until she'd given him a piece of her mind.

"Where is he?" she asked. "Where's Shane? Is he still in jail?"

"No," Gretchen said. "Everly bailed them out. I'm assuming she took them to the parsonage. Shane didn't look like he was in any condition to drive back to Dallas. He seemed a little out of it."

Delaney turned and headed for the door, but Stetson jumped up and beat her to it.

"Just take a second to calm down, Delaney. I think the Kingmans have done enough to Shane."

"And I don't think they've done near enough."

"Del—"

Uncle Jack cut in. "Let her go, Stetson. Delaney's a big girl. She can handle this."

Stetson hesitated for a moment before he stepped out of her way.

It didn't take Delaney long to get into town. By the time she got to the parsonage, she had worked herself into a fine temper. She banged on the door, uncaring that it was so early in the morning. She expected Chance or Shane to answer. Instead, Everly did. The woman even looked stunning in baggie sweats with bad bed-head. She yawned widely when she saw Delaney and stretched her arms over her head, showing off a flat stomach and a belly button ring.

"Well, howdy, cowgirl."

Delaney scowled. "Where is Shane?"

"He's still sleeping after our night of hot sex."

The shaft of pain that pierced Delaney's heart had her physically flinching.

Everly rolled her eyes. "I'm kidding. Shane and I haven't had hot sex for years." That did not make Delaney feel better. "After I bailed him and Chance out of jail, he kept me up all night whining about you."

Delaney blinked. "About me?"

Everly shook her head. "You two are so clueless." When Delaney narrowed her eyes, she held up her hands. "Don't go all country postal on me. I just think that anyone with half a brain can see Shane is crazy about you."

"If he's so crazy about me, why did he leave? And what was he doing drinking shots with you last night while I was . . ."

"Crying your eyes out over breaking your fake engagement?"

Delaney stared at her. "He told you it was fake?"

"The last time I came into town. But I knew even then that what he felt for you was real."

"Then why is he going back to Dallas?"

Everly eyes turned sad. "Because dreams are hard to let go of. Even when the dream is all wrong for you. So give him a better dream, Delaney." She stepped back. "Now if you'll excuse me, I need my beauty rest. Small-town life is much more exciting than I remembered." She started to close the door, but Delaney put her hand out and stopped her.

"But I need to talk to Shane."

"He's not here. He went to church to show support for his brother, who will no doubt be fired by the townsfolk for getting into a bar fight and being tossed into jail." Everly smiled. "I didn't think Mister Holier-Than-Thou had it in him. Now, go get your man, cowgirl. Yeehaw and yippee-ki-yay!" She closed the door.

It looked like the entire town had shown up for church. Even her family. Delaney had no more than pulled into the parking lot, than Buck's truck pulled in behind her, followed by Stetson's and Wolfe's. Thankfully, they didn't ask any questions. They just followed her toward the open front doors. The townsfolk offered up greetings, but Delaney allowed her family to field them. She was too busy looking for Shane.

She found him inside sitting in the Kingman family pew. His face looked as battered as Wolfe's and Buck's. But when he saw her, his soft brown eyes lit up with something that made her heart beat faster.

He got to his feet. "Delaney."

She moved into the pew until they were only inches away. "Shane." There was so much more she wanted to say, but her emotions at seeing him tangled her tongue and all she could do was stand there and stare into his eyes. Shane seemed happy to do the same. They didn't break eye contact until Chance stepped up to the pulpit.

"Good morning. If you could all be seated."

There was a collective gasp from the congregation. When Delaney turned to Chance, she understood why. Chance looked as beat up as Shane and her brothers. It was doubtful the townsfolk would have any trouble figuring out what had happened. In fact, the people who had been at Nasty Jack's last night had probably already spread the gossip this morning—which explained why the church was so full.

Chance knew it too.

"I'm glad to see so many folks here today, but I'm sure you're not here for my eloquent sermons." A commotion at the back of the church had him pausing. Everly came striding down the aisle in a tight lime-green spandex dress that showed off her curvy body and stiletto heels that showed off her long legs.

When she reached the Kingman pew, she muttered a, "Pardon me," then scooted past all of Delaney's family members to squeeze in next to Delaney, forcing her even closer to Shane. Once she was seated, she smiled up at Chance. "You were saying, Preach?"

Chance's jaw tightened before he continued. "As I was saying, I'm sure most of you already know what happened at Nasty Jack's last night. And I owe you an apology. It's my job to set a good example for this congregation. To practice what I preach. Since I didn't do that, I plan to hand in my resig—"

Hester Malone stood up. "Now hold up there,

Pastor. I don't think anyone here is calling for your resignation. I, for one, am happy we have a preacher who understands what it means to be a fallible human being. I think all of us here have lost our temper a time or two and done things we regret."

Kitty Carson jumped up. "I agree."

The entire congregation gasped with surprise. It was the first time Hester and Kitty had agreed on anything. Of course, Kitty couldn't just leave it at that.

She sent Hester a snide look. "And some of us are more fallible than others. Since it looks like whatever went on between the Kingmans and the Ransoms got resolved." She smiled at Delaney and Shane. "And it doesn't look like there's any hard feelings. I think we should just let bygones be bygones. What do ya say, folks?"

The rest of the congregation chimed in with agreement.

"I like a scrappy preacher."

"Nice to have a pastor who can throw a punch."

"A man has to stand up for his family. Didn't Jesus get into it with Peter for talking smack about James?"

Everly pumped a fist in the air and yelled, "Let's keep the pugilist pastor!"

Everyone finally quieted down and waited for Chance to say something, but he seemed speechless at the town's reaction. So Shane got to his feet and spoke.

"I think your generous hearts have left my brother speechless. Thank y'all for being so understanding. I know Chance appreciates your support. And I just want to say that last night was all my fault. I've been a complete and utter idiot and I deserved to get my butt whupped by the Kingmans." He glanced down at Delaney. "I'm sorry I made you cry, Del. I just got scared. I had this plan all laid out and then this sassy cowgirl came along and everything I had worked so hard for didn't seem to matter anymore. Chance brought up that maybe I was worried about letting a woman change my life goals like my mama did with my daddy. And maybe there's some truth to that. But I've come to discover that you're my life goal, Delaney Kingman. Without you I have no life."

It was the sweetest thing Delaney had ever heard in her life. She jumped to her feet and threw her arms around his neck. "Oh, Shane. I love you too. I thought I just wanted a sex partner. But you turned out to be so much more. Hester was right. I didn't get a sexual relationship with you. I got a love connection."

Chance cleared his throat. "Maybe you and Shane should continue this conversation in private."

"Oh, come on, Preach. Let her talk," Everly said. "It looks like all the kids are in Sunday School and this is the best time I've ever had in church."

The congregation laughed. Delaney couldn't help smiling. Everly was growing on her.

Delaney returned her attention to Shane. "I swore I wouldn't fall for my first boyfriend, but how could I not fall for a man who three times a day helped me feed our kids. A man who supported my dream of starting a ranch for abused animals. If you supported my dream, the least I can do is support yours. If you need to be in Dallas, then I'll move to Dallas. I'm sure I can find animals there who need help."

"A Kingman live away from Cursed?" Kitty said. "That don't seem right."

Shane smiled at Delaney. "I'm glad you're willing to move for me, cowgirl. But Miss Kitty has a good point. It wouldn't be right to ask a Kingman to live anywhere but Cursed."

"But what about your dream of becoming a billionaire?"

"Hester also saw my future. She told me that money isn't going to get me what I need most in life." He cradled Delaney's face in his hands. "What I need most is your love, Del. I started falling for you when you beat me so soundly at pool and I just kept on falling the more I got to know you. You are the strongest, kindest, feistiest woman I've ever met. There is nothing fake about the feelings you make me feel." He took her hand and placed it over his heart. She could feel the steady thump beneath her palm. "This is real, Delaney Kingman. And since it's real, I think we need to do it right this time." He got down on one knee. "Will you marry me? I still don't have a ring, but—"

"I got it!" Miss Kitty squeezed past the people in her pew and hurried around the front of the Kingman pew to hand a ring box to Shane.

He opened it and smiled. "Perfect." He held it

up to Delaney. It was a ring made out of a horseshoe nail.

Damned if tears didn't fill her eyes. But she didn't care. She held out her shaking hand and Shane took the ring out of the box and slid it on her finger before he stood and smiled at her.

"I guess it's legit now."

She returned his smile. "I guess it is."

"All you have to do is set the date," Kitty said.

Shane cocked his head. "How about June?"

It seemed like a long time away, but as long as she was with Shane, Delaney could wait. "June of next year is perfect."

His eyes grew confused. "Next year? I was talking about this June."

Delaney stared at him. "But that's only two weeks away."

He grinned. "I hear Kingmans don't have long engagements."

Delaney wrapped her arms around his neck and kissed him. "Damn impatient Kingmans."

Chapter Twenty

"I'M SURPRISED YOU didn't ask me."

Delaney glanced in the bathroom mirror at Mystic, who was braiding her hair. "Ask you what?"

"To read Shane's emotions and tell you what he's feeling."

Delaney smiled. She didn't need Mystic's psychic powers to tell her how Shane felt. She knew he loved her. He'd proven it time and time again in the last two weeks. Not with silly flowers or sappy love notes. He'd proven it with soft kisses and gentle caresses and three words she never grew tired of hearing.

As if reading her thoughts, Mystic returned her smile. "You're right. The man is crazy about you. And you are crazy about him. I hope I find the same kind of love one day."

"You will, Mystic. I thought I'd never be a sappy lovesick fool, but it happened. Now finish up, would ya? I can't take this primping a second longer."

"Hold your water. I'm almost done." Mystic did a little more poking and smoothing before she stepped back. "There." She gave Delaney the hand mirror sitting on the bathroom counter. "What do you think?"

The elaborate French braid Delaney saw in the mirror had her rolling her eyes. "I asked for something simple, Mystic. I didn't want to look like the cartoon version of Rapunzel."

"I loved *Tangled*. What I wouldn't give to get my hands on that head of hair." Mystic adjusted the tiny white flowers she'd woven into the braid before she took the mirror from Delaney and set it down. "And it's your wedding day. You have to go a little over the top on your wedding day. Especially when you refused to wear a dress."

"I'm not a dress kind of gal." She got up from the vanity bench and glanced at her reflection in the bathroom mirror. She thought she looked just right in her new wranglers and flowered western shirt. Even the braid wasn't too bad. Although it would be completely lost beneath her straw cowboy hat—something she wasn't about to mention when Mystic had gone to so much trouble. And maybe it wasn't her hair or her clothes Delaney thought looked so right. Maybe it was the confidence she saw in the eyes that looked back at her. Confidence that hadn't been there a few months earlier.

Delaney Kingman had grown up.

She was no longer the insecure cowgirl who hid behind her family and a false bravado. She was a woman who had fallen in love. Along the way, she'd discovered who she was and what she wanted.

She wanted Shane. But more importantly she wanted a life with him that didn't include a hectic schedule with all work and no play. Or doing what made her siblings happy. But old habits die hard. It hadn't been easy telling Stetson she wasn't going to manage the horse breeding and training at the ranch anymore. Nor had it been easy to tell him that she was using the land Daddy had given her for an abused and neglected animal refuge.

Her concern had been groundless. Stetson had taken both surprisingly well. Probably because he'd already resigned himself to her living in Dallas. But there would be no move to the big city for her. Or for Shane. He had decided he liked living on a ranch surrounded by a big, stubborn, squabbling family and more animals than you could shake a stick at. He still wanted to finish developing his app that would assist seniors and their families with the aging process and Dan Fuller was still on board with financing the project. But Shane no longer spent long hours at his computer. He worked in the mornings, and in the afternoons, he was Delaney's right-hand man.

And she had never had a right-hand man before.

"I'm going to kill that goat!" Buck came striding into the bathroom, holding a new straw hat ... with a big bite taken out of it. Mystic laughed. Which earned her a scowl from Buck. "It's not funny, Missy."

Mystic took the hat and flopped it onto Buck's head, then turned him toward the mirror. "Oh, yeah, it is."

A smile tickled the corners of Buck's mouth.

"Okay, so it's kinda funny. And I guess it wouldn't be Delaney's wedding day if there weren't goats somehow involved." He turned to Delaney. "But I'm not here to talk about what your ornery goat did to my hat. I have a message from the groom. A weird message."

"What is it?" Delaney asked.

"He wants you to wear only one boot. He said you'd know which one. Now how crazy is that?"

A wash of pure happiness welled up inside of Delaney. "Not crazy at all."

Shane couldn't help but smile when Delaney came walking down the rose-strewn aisle in the garden on Stetson's arm. He would remember this day for the rest of his life. Not just because she only wore one boot, but also because of the happiness he read in her eyes. He felt just as happy.

When she reached him, he knelt. She placed a hand on his shoulder as he brushed off her sock and slipped her foot into the boot he'd brought with him. Once it was on, he rose to his feet and looked at his Cinderella.

"Perfect fit."

And she was.

She was the perfect fit for him.

The rest of the wedding ceremony passed in a blur. He answered when Chance asked him questions and repeated when he needed to repeat. But for the most part, all he cared about was the look in Delaney's beautiful blue eyes. A look he wanted to wake up to every morning for the rest of his life.

He only pulled his attention away long enough to slip the engagement ring off her finger and replace it with one made of solid gold. The one she slipped on his finger matched hers. Two horseshoe nail rings for two ranchers.

If someone had told Shane he would one day be a rancher, he would've laughed himself silly. But that's exactly what he had turned into. He mucked out stalls, groomed horses, spread hay, fed goats, and helped Delaney plan her refuge for abused and neglected animals. He'd already set up a website and an app where people could donate. He had a new goal: get a million dollars' worth of donations before the end of the year. He knew he could do it.

"Shane?"

Chance's voice brought Shane out of his musings and he looked at his brother. Shane knew he was still struggling with his grief, but Shane was glad he'd be around to help Chance get over the loss of his wife. And who knew? Maybe Chance would find love again.

"I said you may kiss your bride," Chance said.

"Oh!" Shane looked back at Delaney who was struggling not to laugh. He pulled her into his arms and kissed her. Their relationship had started with a kiss. One kiss and his life had changed forever. Now they were starting their marriage with a kiss. He had a feeling there would be a lot more surprises in store for him with this feisty cowgirl.

The townsfolk's cheers finally pulled them apart and they turned to the people seated in the garden. Everyone from Cursed was there. Shane never thought he'd live in a small town. But as he walked Delaney down the aisle and through the sea of smiling faces, he couldn't help thinking that a small town was the best place to live.

For the next half hour, the photographer took numerous shots of him and Delaney around the ranch. Then Chance and the entire Kingman clan joined in. Shane had grown up with a grandma and a brother. Now he had a gruff uncle and more siblings than he'd ever imagined. After the photographer was finished, the entire family headed to the barn where everyone from town was waiting. As per Delaney's wishes, barbecue ribs and chicken, corn on the cob, potato salad, ranch-style beans, and watermelon filled the long tables covered in checkered tablecloths. For dessert there was no cake, just plenty of Gretchen's pies.

Gretchen had stacked three apple pies on a tiered tray and Delaney and Shane cut into the top pie and then took turns cramming pieces of it into each other's mouths. They danced the first dance to Blake Shelton's "God Gave Me You."

Delaney cried.

"You've turned me into a watering pot," she complained with a sniff.

Shane brushed the tears from her cheeks. "I like when you show me all your emotions."

"In that case, I'm going to show you my impatience. I don't want to stay here for more dancing. I'm ready to be alone with you."

He felt the same way. "Then let's get out of

here." He glanced over at Buck, who was waltzing with Mystic. "Buck! It's time."

Buck stopped dancing and headed out of the barn.

"What was that all about?" Delaney asked.

"You'll see soon enough." He whirled her under his arm and continued to dance her around the floor. They danced one more dance before Buck showed back up.

"Everything's set," Buck said with a wink.

Before Delaney could start asking questions again, Shane led her out of the barn where two horses waited. Mutt for Delaney and the sweet mare Shane had been practicing on for the last two weeks.

"What—" Delaney started, but he placed a finger against her lips.

"Just trust me."

Even though his cowgirl didn't need any help, he helped her into the saddle before he moved to his horse. Delaney watched with concerned eyes. But she didn't say a word as he mounted and took the reins. Because he knew where they were going, he led the way . . . and showed off a little bit. He guided the horse into a trot before he slowed back down to a walk. When he glanced over, the look on Delaney's face in the moonlight made all the hours of practice worthwhile. Her eyes held love and pride.

She smiled. "Hey, cowboy."

He grinned. "Hey, cowgirl."

With locked gazes, they rode alongside each other for a few more minutes before Delaney spoke. "So now that you've given me the best wedding present a girl could ask for, you want to go back to the castle and do a little more ridin'?"

"Oh, we're going to do a little more riding. But we're not going back to the castle." He put his heels to the mare and took off. Mutt had no problem keeping up and Shane knew Delaney held him back to stay neck and neck with the mare. When they reached the copse of trees, Shane reined in and dismounted. He helped Delaney dismount before he took her reins and tied both horses to a mesquite bush. Buck would be there to pick them up soon.

Taking Delaney's hand, he led her to the tree house. When she saw the white twinkle lights he, Buck, Stetson, Gage, and Wolfe had strung up in the tree, she halted in her tracks.

"Oh, Shane. It's beautiful."

"You haven't seen the best part." He lifted her into his arms and carried her up the narrow stairs. The door was cracked open. He figured Adeline, Gretchen, and Lily must've left it ajar. While the Kingman men had helped him with the outside, the Kingman women had helped him with the inside.

He pushed open the door and stepped inside.

More twinkle lights hung along the top of the walls and around the windows. An ice bucket with a bottle of champagne and two fluted glasses sat on the small table. In the middle of the mattress, Shane had painstakingly placed a heart made of red rose petals.

Except the heart wasn't a heart anymore and

only a few rose petals remained. The culprits stood on the mattress munching away. Shane wasn't surprised to see Karl. The goat got out on a regular basis and wandered everywhere on the ranch. But he *was* surprised to see a baby goat with three black stockings.

He was about to get after Karl and Dopey when Delaney kissed him. The kind of kiss that erased all thoughts from a man's head. When she drew back, her eyes were glittering with unshed tears.

"Thank you."

He set her on her feet and pulled her close. "I wanted tonight to be a night you'd remember."

She gave him a wide-eyed look. "Are you sure? I mean the first time with a married woman should be special. I don't know if you can handle the responsibility. What if I should fall even more in love with you?"

His heart burst to overflowing as he leaned in to kiss her. "That's a chance I'm willing to take."

THE END

Turn the page for a **Special Sneak Peek** of the next **Kingman Ranch** novel!

SNEAK PEEK!
Charming a Texas Prince
Coming October, 2022!

SHE WOULD NEVER admit it. And if asked, Mystic Twilight Malone would flat-out deny that the second Wednesday was her favorite day of the month.

It was just a day like any other day.

She got up at exactly six fifteen. She did yoga for thirty minutes. She mediated for ten minutes more. Then she showered and got dressed. If she took a little extra time picking out her clothes or fixing her hair or applying her makeup, she didn't give it a thought. It was part of her job to look nice for her clients. A hair stylist needed to have style.

Once she was satisfied with the reflection in her mirror, she'd go into the kitchen and make hot tea for her grandmother. There was a specific routine her grandmother had taught her to make the perfect cup of tea. Always use filtered water and loose tea leaves. And always let the tea steep for five minutes.

After pouring water over the infuser filled with leaves, Mystic would set the timer on her smart watch. While waiting, she'd toast an English muffin lightly brown and spread butter into every nook and cranny. By that time, her alarm would go off and she would remove the tea infuser and then carry the cup and the muffin to the small two-person table in the breakfast nook where she would leave it for her grandmother.

Mystic didn't like tea. Or English muffins. She usually just made herself a cup of black coffee. Except on the second Wednesday of every month. On those days, she just sat at the table and stared out the window, waiting for the clock to tick off time.

For some reason, the second Wednesday of every month always turned out to be a gorgeous day. The sun seemed to shine even brighter. The rain fell even lovelier. The hailstones danced in the grass even prettier.

Nothing that happened that day could ruin her good mood. It didn't matter if her beauty supply shipment didn't come in. Or a client didn't show up for their appointment. Or her grandmother had caused another problem with the townsfolk of Cursed, Texas. Regardless of what happened, the second Wednesday of every month always turned out to be a great day.

Even if her grandmother woke up spouting predictions.

"Tornado's coming."

Mystic continued watching the hummingbirds sipped from the feeder that hung outside the window. Was it her imagination or were the two birds kissing after every drink? She smiled at the thought of hummingbirds kissing.

"H-h-humph. It must be the second Wednesday."

Mystic turned to her grandmother. "What?"

"Nothing." Hester sat down at the table. She was a tall, attractive woman with long silver hair that she refused to let Mystic cut—no matter how much Mystic pleaded. She also refused to wear any color but black—no matter how many brightly colored clothes Mystic gave her for her birthdays and Christmases. The long silver hair and black, flowing dresses and skirts only added to the townsfolk beliefs that Hester Malone was a witch. And her grandmother's career choice didn't help. Mystic cringed every time she saw the neon sign hanging in the front window of their house.

FORTUNETELLING AND PALM READING.

Like her ancestors before her, Hester was the town psychic. She read palms and tarot cards and crystal balls and the amethyst hanging from the chain around her neck. If her predictions of doom-and-gloom weren't accurate more than eighty percent of the time, people might not believe she was a witch. But Hester was rarely wrong.

"Did you hear me?" Her grandmother took a seat across from Mystic and picked up her favorite tea mug with the picture of Baby Yoda and the words *Yoda Best Psychic* beneath. "A tornado is coming."

"I heard you." Mystic glanced out the window at the beautiful August day. "But not only is it a gorgeous day, tornado season for Texas is usually May and early June."

Hester added four cubes of sugar to her tea and stirred it six times one way and four times the other before setting the spoon on the table. "The tornadoes in my dream don't always represent actual tornadoes. You should know that by now, Granddaughter."

Mystic more than knew it. Hester hadn't just taught her how to make tea. She'd taught her everything she knew about the psychic world. More than Mystic wanted to know. Her grandmother's dreams, visions, and the other psychic abilities had caused Mystic nothing but trouble and alienation from the townsfolk. What Hester viewed as a gift, Mystic viewed as a curse. She wasn't about to give her validation by entering into a conversation about some dream she had.

"I don't want to talk about dreams, Hessy. That's something *you* should know by now, Grandmother."

Hester slammed her fist on the table, making her tea mug jump. "This isn't a joke, Mystic Twilight! Something bad is going to happen to you. I know it."

"How do you know it? You told me yourself that Malones can't read each other's fortunes or see the future of any blood relative."

"The dream didn't go into detail. It was just a warning. A serious warning." Tears entered her violet eyes. Eyes that Mystic had inherited. "I can't lose you like I lost your mama."

The tears and the mention of Aurora made Mystic realize how upset her grandmother was by the dream. Hester rarely cried and even more rarely talked about her only daughter who had disappeared from both their lives when Mystic was only three years old.

Mystic reached across the table and took Hester's hand. "Okay. I'm listening. What kind of tornado is coming?"

Hester stroked the amethyst crystal around her neck. "That's just it. I don't know if it's literal or metaphorical. All I saw in my dream was a tornado headed straight for you. Your hair was whipping around your face and you were scared. More scared than I've ever seen you."

She squeezed her grandmother's hand. "If it's an actual tornado, I couldn't work anywhere better than my basement salon. If it's a sign of something that's going to happen in my life, I'll just have to deal with it when it hits."

Hester's eyes grew even more concerned. "That's the problem. You never deal with issues. You just hide from them. Just like your mama did."

"My mama didn't hide. She ran. I'm not a runner, Hessy." If she had been, she would've left a long time ago. Leaving would've made her life so much easier. But she couldn't bring herself to leave Hester. As much as her grandmother annoyed her, Mystic loved her and owed her for being there when her mother hadn't been. "I promise I'll keep my eyes open and take all the precautions I need to if a tornado—real or otherwise—shows up in my life."

"And you'll keep me posted on anything unusual that happens?" Hester asked. "I mean it, Mystic. I can't help you if you continue to keep secrets from me."

She took note of the "continue," but refused to acknowledge it. She had kept a secret from her grandmother. And everyone else in town.

"I'll keep you posted." She added a silent amendment. *If it's something I think you need to know.* Mystic got up. "Now stop worrying. I'm going to be fine."

"I don't want you to be fine. I want you to be happy."

"I am happy."

Hester shook her head. "You can fool the townsfolk, but you can't fool me. You haven't been truly happy since high school. Something happened back then. Something that took your sparkle away. If there wasn't a psychic block with my own family members, I would've known what it was and I could've helped you." She hesitated. "I still can if you'd tell me."

Mystic thanked God everyday for the family psychic block. Hester didn't need to know what had happened. She would only try to help and cause more problems.

"There's nothing to tell." She brushed a kiss on Hester's cheek before she grabbed a banana from the bowl on the counter and headed out the front door. As she was coming down the porch steps, her cat Wish popped out from beneath the azaleas and greeted her with a loud meow. "There you are. Out carousing again last night, were you?" she said as she leaned down to stroke the cat's sleek black fur.

Mystic had sworn she would never get another cat after Magic—the cat her grandmother had given her on her tenth birthday—had died. Not only did she not want to feel the sharp pain of loss again, but she also didn't want to add to the townsfolk's belief that the Malone women were witches. But then Wish had shown up on her doorstep a few months back and she'd been unable to turn the cat away.

"Come on," she said. "I'll get you some breakfast."

The cat daintily followed behind her as she headed down the steps to the basement door.

Stepping into the salon always filled Mystic with pride. She had designed every aspect of the salon herself. She'd picked out the striped lavender wallpaper and cushioned purple salon chairs and black and white checkered tile and the black shampoo bowls and the chrome fixtures and the white lobby couch and each fuzzy pillow.

She loved everything about the salon. This was her haven. The place where she wasn't the granddaughter of the town fortuneteller and palm reader. Or the poor parentless Malone girl whose mama had run off and left her. Here, she was just a prominent businesswoman who had worked hard to get the town's respect. She was damn proud of her accomplishment.

After feeding Wish, she started getting the salon

open for business. She set up the cash register and arranged the magazines on the coffee table in front of the lobby couch. She pulled the clean towels out of the dryer and folded them before stacking them back in the cupboards over the shampoo bowls. She swept the floor for any hair she might've missed the night before.

Once everything was ready, she put away the broom and dustpan and glanced at the clock on the wall.

9:07

She smiled.

Her first appointment on the second Wednesday of every month was always late. She walked to the mirror at her station and reapplied her favorite brand of red lipstick before she fluffed her short black hair and brushed a fleck of mascara from beneath her eye.

When the bell over the door jingled, her heart rate accelerated. She ignored her heart. Just like she would continue to ignore it for the next hour.

She turned from the mirror as her morning appointment strode in. He wore the light blue t-shirt with the Austin brewpub logo on the front and his favorite pair of faded wranglers with the worn spot on the right back pocket. His straw cowboy hat was new. His sister Delaney's goat Karl had munched on the last one ... and the one before that ... and the one before that. Beneath the curved brim, his familiar cobalt blue eyes twinkled back at her.

"Hey, Missy!"

She placed a hand on her hip in faked exasperation. "You're late again, Buck Kingman."

"Sorry. Big brother called me into his office and got after me for being forgetful." He hooked his cowboy hat on the coat rack before he walked over and handed her a takeout cup. "But I didn't forget your coffee."

She took a sip and sighed. "Then you're forgiven."

He laughed as he folded his tall frame into the salon chair at her station. "I wish my brother was so easy to appease."

Paying absolutely no attention to the way his muscled body filled the chair, Mystic sat down her coffee at her station and took a purple plastic cape from a drawer. She shook it out before placing it around Buck's broad shoulders. The sight of the rough and tough cowboy in a purple cape always made her smile.

"So what did you forget this time?" she asked. Buck had always been disorganized and forgetful. He was lucky he had four older siblings to keep him on track. And Mystic. "I told you to start using your cellphone calendar to give you reminder alerts."

"I know. I know. But I never had to remember to schedule the hay crew. One of my siblings always did that. Now, suddenly, it's my job."

She snapped the cape around his neck, ignoring the feel of the warm skin on the back of his neck. "Your sisters and brothers have other responsibilities. Like their new spouses."

Buck scowled. "Exactly."

"It sounds a little like you're jealous."

"Hell yeah, I'm jealous. I'm the one in the family who always wanted to get married. And now everyone is married but me. It doesn't seem fair."

Since they'd been in high school, the only thing Buck had ever dreamed about was getting married and having a bunch of kids. At one time, Mystic had wanted the same thing. Now she was quite happy being a single, prosperous businesswoman.

Quite happy.

"Poor Buck," she said as she picked up a comb from her station. "You live in a castle on a hill and can have any woman in town you want, but it's still not enough."

He shot her an annoyed look. "I should've know I wouldn't get any sympathy from you."

"Not a drop." Mystic ran the comb through his hair.

It was the color of moonlight. And in bright sunlight, it almost looked like he wore a glowing halo. But she knew for a fact that Buck was no angel. At eight, he'd almost burned the barn down due to his infatuated with matches and fire. At thirteen, he'd stolen Wolfe's girlie magazines and barricaded himself in the tree house for hours. At fifteen, he'd written the answers to his history final on the inside of his arm. At seventeen, he'd had sex with Ginny Myers in her bedroom while her parents were downstairs watching the Big Bang Theory. As an adult, he drank, gambled, cussed and fought when provoked . . . and continued to entertain women in their bedrooms.

No, Buck wasn't an angel. But he was a good-hearted man who would make some woman a great husband.

Just not her.

She stopped combing his hair and stepped back. "So you want the same cut as usual or would you like to try something daring." She cocked her head and sent him a sassy look in the mirror. "Maybe a mullet? Or I could shave the words, 'Marry Me' in the back."

Buck laughed. He had the best laugh. A chortle mixed with a loud guffaw. "If you think it would help, shave away."

"That desperate, are you?"

His laughter quickly died and a sadness entered his blue eyes. "Why can't I find love, Miss? All my siblings have found it and they weren't even looking. I've been looking for years and it's completely eluded me." His gaze held her in its grip. "Am I that ugly?"

Ugly? Buck Kingman was about as far from ugly as a man could get. It wasn't just his blond hair that sprout from his head like a field of moonlit wheat. Or his straight nose without one bump or freckle to mar it. Or his wide mouth with two even twin peaks on top and a plump full lip on the bottom he chewed on when he got worried. Or his deep blue eyes with their long golden lashes. Or the cute little dimple in his left cheek that came out when he smiled his lopsided grin. It was the combination of all those features wrapped in a muscled cowboy's body that made all the women in town breathless. Including her. She had just learned to regulate her breathing when he was around.

She, playfully, tapped him on the head with the comb. "You're not so ugly, Buckaroo. I'm sure some woman somewhere will find you cute enough to fall head over boots in love with you. Now let's get your hair washed. I've got other clients today."

"Gee, thanks for the pep talk, Miss," he said sarcastically as he got up from the chair and followed her to the shampoo bowl.

Once he had reclined in the chair with his head position in the curve of the sink, she picked up the sprayer and wet his hair before applying a liberal amount of conditioning shampoo. As soon as she slid her fingers into his hair and started to massage his scalp, his eyes slid closed like they always did.

She glanced at the clock.

This was her moment. The one moment once a month that she let down her guard. The one moment when she stepped across the line drawn in the sand of her heart and let herself feel.

As her fingers stroked through Buck's sudsy strands, her heart quickened and her breath grew uneven and she pretended for a second they were different people. Two strangers with no past and no history. Two strangers who could start all over and maybe this time find love.

She only gave herself the minute. No more. And no less. She felt like a minute wasn't too much to ask for. Once it was up, she removed her fingers and rinsed the shampoo.

By the time Buck opened his eyes, all he saw was his smiling best friend.

(Charming a Texas Prince Excerpt by Katie Lane)

PREORDER NOW!
https://katielanebooks.com/index.php/series/kingman-ranch

Other Titles by Katie Lane

Be sure to check out all of Katie Lane's novels!
www.katielanebooks.com

Kingman Ranch Series
Charming a Texas Beast
Charming a Knight in Cowboy Boots
Charming a Big Bad Texan
Charming a Fairytale Cowboy
Charming a Texas Prince (October 2022)

Bad Boy Ranch Series:
Taming a Texas Bad Boy
Taming a Texas Rebel
Taming a Texas Charmer
Taming a Texas Heartbreaker
Taming a Texas Devil
Taming a Texas Rascal
Taming a Texas Tease
Taming a Texas Christmas Cowboy

Brides of Bliss Texas Series:
Spring Texas Bride
Summer Texas Bride
Autumn Texas Bride
Christmas Texas Bride

Tender Heart Texas Series:
Falling for Tender Heart

Falling Head Over Boots
Falling for a Texas Hellion
Falling for a Cowboy's Smile
Falling for a Christmas Cowboy

Deep in the Heart of Texas Series:
Going Cowboy Crazy
Make Mine a Bad Boy
Catch Me a Cowboy
Trouble in Texas
Flirting with Texas
A Match Made in Texas
The Last Cowboy in Texas
My Big Fat Texas Wedding

Overnight Billionaires Series:
A Billionaire Between the Sheets
A Billionaire After Dark
Waking up with a Billionaire

Hunk for the Holidays Series:
Hunk for the Holidays
Ring in the Holidays
Unwrapped

About the Author

KATIE LANE IS a firm believer that love conquers all and laughter is the best medicine. Which is why you'll find plenty of humor and happily-ever-afters in her contemporary and western contemporary romance novels. A USA Today Bestselling Author, she has written numerous series, including *Deep in the Heart of Texas, Hunk for the Holidays, Overnight Billionaires, Tender Heart Texas, The Brides of Bliss Texas, Bad Boy Ranch,* and *Kingman Ranch.* Katie lives in Albuquerque, New Mexico, and when she's not writing, she enjoys reading, eating chocolate (dark, please), and snuggling with her high school sweetheart and Cairn Terrier, Roo.

For more on her writing life or just to chat,
check out Katie here:
Facebook *www.facebook.com/katielaneauthor*
Instagram *www.instagram.com/katielanebooks*

And for information on upcoming releases and great giveaways, be sure to sign up for her mailing list at *www.katielanebooks.com*!